A MODERN-DAY ROGUE

A smooth-talking negotiator, Jared Cassidy does multimillion-dollar deals for breakfast…and any number of women in between. What he can't handle? His mother. And in a moment of insanity he told her he's finally found a bride.

AND AN OLD-FASHIONED WALLFLOWER

More than anyone, romance-novel addict Violet Murphy knows where her rakish boss has been. That's why she's steered clear. But now, having accepted a proposal that's only moderately less indecent than usual, she has two choices: Spend two steamy and lavishly paid weeks as the pretend fiancée of a playboy no woman has truly ever understood, or use the time in Palm Beach to kill the image and reveal the man. In doing the latter, she'll find paradise, passion, and the promise of a future she's only ever imagined.

KILLING CASANOVA

Kary Rader

DataMatch Success Story No. 4

www.BOROUGHSPUBLISHINGGROUP.com

KILLING CASANOVA

ISBN 978-1-942886-53-2

For those who found true love and lost it...and to those still searching.

CONTENTS

KILLING CASANOVA

Chapter One

Violet

"You bastard."

He slowly looked up and drank her in, if one could drink with their gaze. And Alexander could. Oh. He could.

Eleanor steeled herself against the onslaught of lust and love in her own chest. "You would have let me go? Let me marry someone else?"

"You do realize I'm standing here, right?"

I gritted my teeth, not looking up from the paperback. "It's a good part. Let me finish."

His body was frozen in place but his eyes—

"Why do you read that crap?"

I sighed. "Because I find it entertaining and informative." I bent my head and held the book more tightly.

—his eyes burned with the same lust and love. "I still would let you marry someone else if that was what you wanted, Eleanor. I only want to give you that which you want. But you've come back. Why?"

"I can be entertaining and informative too, you know." The deep sexy voice burred down at me.

I licked my lips but still didn't meet his gaze. "Hmm. Tempting. But I prefer my heroes to have at least two dimensions."

Her heart ached and trembled with overwhelming love and affection, with everlasting devotion. She'd come to tell him how she felt. She would tell him. She must tell him. And he must hear her heart's cry.

My desk shifted with his weight. "Can't imagine any circumstance in any other company where this would be okay."

I could see his form in my peripheral vision and could feel the warmth of his body as he leaned over me. My heart began to traitorously thump as it always did when he was this close. "If you made it to work more often, maybe I wouldn't have to read to occupy myself." I tamped down my emotion and blocked him out for the sake of Alexander and Eleanor.

The words somehow formed on her lips and Eleanor's voice gained strength from her beating heart. "Alexander, I love—"

The phone rang.

"Shit." I frowned and slapped the book down, finally glancing up at the man standing in front of my desk. "Now I won't get to finish until break."

I snatched the receiver while at last allowing my eyes to wander his dark features, my heart thumping in response. "Jared Cassidy's office."

The very same stood right there in front of me looking for all the world like a Harlequin Billionaire Hero, which he actually kind of was. His liquid chocolate eyes met mine and a shiver rolled down my spine just like it always did. The romance abruptly vanished as a shrill voice screeched in my ear.

"Is Jared in yet? This is Lori."

I winced at the painful timber. "Good morning, Lori." I glared up at the scoundrel in question, because distain had become my defense against a man who could charm the panties off Mother Theresa, even if she was dead. His eyes went with wide with terror, and he shook his head pleadingly.

I narrowed my glare to slits of disapproval then lied. "I'm sorry. Mr. Cassidy hasn't made it into the office yet."

It was nearly noon.

"That *bastard*," she screeched.

Shades of *Ravished by a Rogue* came back in fits of déjà vu via Lori's squeaky pitch. I inwardly groaned. Had Jared really slept with this woman? Well, technically I doubted they slept, and I knew from the myriad of daily messages that he rarely, if ever, spent the entire night—

"He told me he was going straight to work." Lori's nails-on-a-chalkboard caterwauling cut off my ruminations and ground down into the crevices of my mind, threatening to pop my eyes from their sockets. "If he's with that tramp Lenore Echols, I'll yank those strawberry-blonde extensions right out of her specially treated scalp."

Jared choked on a laugh, apparently catching her verbiage from where he stood. His forehead furrowed, but his eyes held unrepentant humor. I should tell the woman he'd just walked in and let him deal with her. They didn't pay me enough to deal with this crap.

Actually, that wasn't true. SC Endeavors paid me quite well to babysit the vice president and chief operating officer, and if I wanted to keep making my vulgar wages, I had to take care of Jared's vulgar crap…like *Lori*.

I wanted to snarl at him but instead I shook my head in resignation, knowing what I had to do. "I believe Mr. Cassidy is meeting with a business associate this morning." I bared my teeth and narrowed my eyes, hating to lie for a second time. But the truth wouldn't benefit any of the involved parties. Especially not me and my tattered eardrum.

"Fine." She huffed, sounding like silverware scraped across a china plate. "Have him call me as soon as he gets in."

I winced and a wave of pity swept over me. Poor Lori, one more in an endless stream of broken hearts. Possessive was one thing anyone with a brain knew you should never be with Jared "Casanova" Cassidy, but that didn't stop women from trying. And for what? A man they knew would never really love them? A man who could never be faithful? Talk about an exercise in futility.

"I'll be sure to do that." I tried to add some cheer to my voice, but that was hard with a scowl on my face. I set the receiver down and crossed my arms over my chest. "So where have you been exactly?"

He flashed me a roguish grin, again reminding me of my book hero. "Do you really want to know the answer to that, Vi?"

No, I didn't. The extra thump in my heart was still there, but it was easier to control when I got to see inside his real life. It made distancing myself that much easier. It just wasn't fair that he should be so dang attractive, and such a horn dog. I rolled my eyes. "Mr. Tate called. His report's on your desk. Mr. Scorge was looking for you."

He absently fingered a file I was working on, making even the simplest of gestures seem…sexual, dang it.

"Nathaniel is always looking for me." He propped a hip on the edge of my desk again. "What did Tate want?"

"He wants to schedule a meeting with you for the DataMatch rollout. And he wants to meet with Maddie before…*you know*."

DataMatch was all anyone in the company could talk about anymore. Maybe because without it there would be no company. But very few in the office really knew the truth. Sure, rumors about an in-house test pilot ran rampant. People always came to me with their theories. Theories I could neither deny nor confirm. Even though *I* knew the truth.

The truth of the test pilot was that five people had been hired to date their bosses and test the accuracy of the matchmaking software before it was released to the public.

I myself had been counted in that number but, naturally, my boss had made it clear he didn't want to seriously date anyone, especially not me. And I didn't want to have sex on his desk—because God only knew how many others had been there before. I also didn't want to become one of the "pitiful assistants," as they were called. The women in the office whom Jared seduced and then tossed to the curb. Those poor fools ended up crying in the women's bathroom before being sent away with undisclosed amounts of severance for their troubles.

But there was real trouble in my heart of hearts. I knew somewhere deep in my knower that this man had been made for me—at least he had before he'd been broken. Something had happened to Jared. I didn't know what, but more than anything I wanted to find out. Only that was impossible now, and I couldn't foresee a time and place where it could actually happen. What I did know was that if I ever broke down and slept with him, my heart would be lost. And as for an actual future with my "perfect match"? I had a paper prayer in the fiery pits of hell of that happening.

Just because Jared and I were a bust in the DataMatch test pilot didn't mean everyone was. Two of the five couples had extremely successful results. Less than a year later, they were already engaged to be married.

But there had been one serious misstep with the test pilot. Maddie Timms, the CEO's admin-turned-girlfriend, had another, better match than her boss, Nathaniel Scorge. Unfortunately, that other man, Lewis Tate, was, in a recent business deal with SC Endeavors, contractually guaranteed his "perfect match": Maddie.

Upon discovering the blunder, Mr. Scorge had demanded that in-house counsel oppose the contract and its obligations. The case, which could have ruined the company, ultimately ended in mediation, with Lewis Tate being guaranteed the right to begin a dating relationship with Maddie sometime during the winter holidays. Let's just say that the grumpy bear CEO was none too happy about his girlfriend being forced to date another man.

"God, why doesn't Tate give it up? Maddie will never choose him over Nathaniel." Jared rubbed his face, pulling his freshly shaven skin taut. "This is why I never do emotional entanglements. Get the man on the line. I assume that's what Nathaniel wants to talk to me about." He shook his head sympathetically. "Poor bastard."

Jared and Mr. Scorge had been friends since childhood. I nodded sympathetically.

"Nathaniel drunk dialed me last night."

I winced, trying to imagine the formidable and taciturn CEO even knowing how to drunk dial. "He just needs to trust Maddie. I know she loves him."

"You don't understand, Vi. He's never been this vulnerable. At least not for a very long time." Jared picked up my *Fifty Shades of Grey* paperweight. He frowned and a pensive finger tapped the object. "I'd never let myself get in that deep. Love and romance— it's all bullshit. Doesn't exist."

I knew that was partly the truth, and on one level I agreed with him. I wouldn't give my heart away to just anyone, and so far, no one I'd ever met had earned the privilege. But that didn't mean, by extension, I would never give it away. I would. Eventually. However, the man had to be the right one. My heart thumped again. *No. That man is the wrong one.*

Jared replaced the paperweight and thumbed through my novel. He lowered his eyelids to half-mast, and his voice took on a husky quality. "I could show you as good a time as anything in those storybooks you're reading, Vi."

I snorted, trying to keep my hormones to a less-than-radioactive level. The images that he conjured with just his voice were enough to pump ten pounds of molten desire through my veins. "But your brand of romance doesn't come with a built-in happily ever after."

This wasn't the first time Jared had propositioned me. My boss had made it more than clear that, while he wouldn't entertain the possibility of a dating relationship, he would more than consider a physical liaison. My heart thundered in my chest. *Traitor.*

I snatched the book out of his reach, placing it in my lap drawer for safe keeping before standing and taking a step back from my desk. "Janice, Marcy, Gail, and *Lori* have all called this morning." If that wasn't an answer to—and an indictment of—his indecent proposal, I didn't know what was.

With no small amount of drama, he sighed, giving up his pursuit for the time being.

In the last six months I'd learned how to read Jared Cassidy. His charm and easy smile put him on the watch list of every female in his path. But it was all a cover up for something—something I couldn't quite get a handle on. One thing I knew: He was insulating himself with all these girls just like I was insulating myself with my romance novels. But the real question was why. Why was he hiding behind a string of one-night stands?

Somehow, if I could find the answer to that burning question, I could unlock—

Idiot. I wasn't a heroine on a treasure quest, and I would never be. This was real life and Jared was a real man—i.e., not romance hero material.

Taking a fortifying breath, I followed him into his office and dropped his correspondence into his overflowing inbox. "Can you please sign these letters today so I don't have to redo the dates again?"

He plopped down in his leather chair, tipping it as far back as it could go without toppling. "Anything else, Mother?"

"Oh crap. I almost forgot: Did you call your mom?"

His tanned face drained of color and he jerked up straight. "When did she call?" Deep creases furrowed his brow, and tight, white lines formed at his mouth. "Why didn't you tell me?"

Startled by the censure lacing his voice, I stepped back. I'd worked for Jared for nearly nine months, and I'd never seen him like this. Anxiety gripped my gut. Was he about to fire me? He threatened to do it all the time, but that was playful banter. This was real anger. "I-I sent a text like you asked."

He scrambled for his phone and scrolled through what I was sure were at least a hundred text messages from women. He found mine and sighed. Then he hit the call button without glancing back at me.

"Hey, old lady, you called for a mechanic? Yeah, yeah. I know I'm your favorite son."

He looked up and dismissed me with his eyes, the hardness seeping through.

My head pulsed and my heart still drummed out a disconcerted beat. I hastily retreated to my desk but left my novel in the drawer and began typing.

Chapter Two

Jared

I held the phone in a death grip as I watched Violet retreat to her desk like a skittish kitten. I'd been too harsh. *Fuck.* I was never harsh…well, except when they wanted me to be. But I never wanted to be with her. If it weren't for Violet, Nathaniel would've kicked me to the curb by now. How had I managed before her?

"Hello, honey." Mom's tired voice rang weakly in my ear.

I sank back into my chair, dread clenching deep in my gut. "You sound like you had a long night of drinking and carousing again."

"Oh yeah. You know me. I'm one harebrained episode away from rehab."

I chuckled, letting her humor calm my building tension. Truth: I was the one who needed a drink…or seven. Or even rehab. Silence lingered on the line for a fraction too long, the reason for her call clear.

Finally, she said, "I've heard from the doctor."

Bands of fear tightened around my chest. My eyes stung. Goddammit. I forced in a breath as I pictured her sitting on the couch in the living room. She'd be in her cotton pajamas, a cup of coffee and the morning paper on the table in front of her. Her bald head would be covered with some god-awful scarf regurgitated from the seventies, and she'd be biting her fingernails. I forced charm into my words. "And what did he say?"

"He's setting me up with hospice. Mari and I met with the three nurses today."

I dropped my head, all the breath leaving me in a gut punch. Hospice was tantamount to a death sentence. I imagined the conversation with the doctor. *"Sorry, Ms. Cassidy, there's nothing else we can do but make you comfortable."* They always said shit like that. *"Let us make you comfortable."* I didn't want her to be comfortable—I wanted her to be well!

"I'm flying down there and packing you up. You're moving here. We can get a second opinion. There are plenty of—"

"Jared."

I lumbered on. "—quality treatment centers—"

"Jared."

I forced the giant knot from my throat, but the weight of a rhino still sank into my chest.

"I don't want to move. I want to stay right here…for however long."

For however long? This wasn't happening. I squeezed my eyes and pinched my nose. "I'll take a leave—"

"Mari's here and taking good care of me," she interrupted.

My older sister would definitely do that, but I wanted to go to her. To be there for her. I knew very well she wouldn't let me. She wouldn't want to be a bother. As if that were possible. Catherine Cassidy could never be a bother to anyone—especially not to me. My eyes burned and stung with tears, but I refused to use one of the tissues I reserved for the pitiful ones. I swore under my breath, cursing my father. He was the one who should be there.

The man had left when I was four. I barely remembered him, although I apparently looked a lot like him. In pictures I supposed I could see a resemblance. Never married to my mother, my father had seen our family more as an adventure, an exercise in domestication that didn't work. So he left, and we hadn't seen or heard from him since.

In my last memory of Alejandro Vega, he was wearing a tan suit with a blue T-shirt. Like a bad extra on *Miami Vice,* he wore no socks with his docksiders. He'd patted me on the head, slung the leather duffle over his shoulder, and walked out. Mom had sat with Mari in the kitchen, both of them crying. I'd watched him drive away from our small home in West Palm Beach, and I'd never forgiven him. I never would.

A man didn't make promises or children he couldn't keep. I never made promises to anyone. And I'd never made kids. That had always been my code, and I'd kept it. It was protected sex or nothing. Well, sometimes I settled for oral.

"I thought I'd have more time. I thought I'd live to see you"— her voice broke—"settled with a family of your own."

Mom's voice jerked me back to present day. Oh shit. *Settled? With a family?* Tension built a high rise on top of my anxiety.

"I wanted so much for you to find love, sweetheart, but I see now the scars your father left are too deep."

My double espresso churned in my stomach. My heart struggled against an invisible band tightening around it. I squeezed my eyes closed and shit just spewed from my mouth. "I have a girlfriend."

"What?"

What had I said? Holy hell. I sucked in a breath, trying not to completely lose hold of the shards of my mind I had left.

"A real girlfriend, Jared? Is that true?"

The wonder and hope in her voice left me no choice. "Yeah, Mom. It's true. I didn't want to say anything until I knew for sure, but she's the one. We haven't made it official yet, but—"

"Oh God, Jared. You're serious. You're really serious. Who is she? What does she look like? Does she have family? Does she live in Chicago?"

A diarrhea stream of inquiries spilled from her. I was going to hell. Young people, this is what lying will get you. "Slow down, Mom. One question at a time."

"When am I going to meet this mystery girl, Jared? It's not like I have a lot of time here, son." She snickered at her little joke.

"That's not funny, and I'm not sure. We're still…working things out." To say the least—the very least. God almighty. I'd created a monster.

"But you said this girl was the one, right?"

The expectation in her voice was too much. I'd been a first-class fiend to tell her I was seriously dating someone, but the woman needed something positive in what little life she had left. My gut twisted again. I knew telling her I had a serious girlfriend was the one thing she wanted to hear. My sister was already happily married, and Mom wanted the same for me. This news was obviously just the thing. She'd perked right up. But now she'd never stop hounding me to meet the mystery woman. I might've bitten off more than I could choke on this time.

"No. You're right. She's the one."

"Well…? When do I get to meet her?"

"Uhh…"

"Jared Michael Cassidy. You haven't even told me her name." She sighed. "Honey, I won't run her off. I just want to meet her. Please let me. I know you're nervous, afraid it won't work out. But even if it doesn't…" Her voice cracked again.

"Okay." A thousand curses formed in my mind. It was a last request. My dying mother's last request. That jackass doctor of hers had been clear on her prognosis. If this last treatment didn't work, her time would be short: three to six months. Not that he truly was a jackass, or incompetent, but he seemed like the best place to fix blame.

"Okay what? Jared? Do I get to meet her or not?"

I almost smiled at the familiar impatience in her voice. "I'll bring her." Christ. What was I saying?

"Really?" The joy and relief in her voice flowed over the phone line.

If I had to pay some actress a million dollars, I'd find someone.

I could imagine the bright smile forming on her lips. My mother was not above playing the cancer card to get what she wanted.

"The Fourth of July Cassidy family reunion is next week. You have to bring her then."

Next week? "I can't find— I mean, I'm not sure she'll be available." I massaged my temples with a thumb and forefinger. My gut was so knotted it would be days before I could eat again.

"Please, Jared. For me. I want to meet her while I'm still feeling human, and not comatose in bed."

"Jesus, Mom. Please don't say that."

"Bring her, Jared."

Surely I could find someone for next week. "All right. I'll see what I can do."

"Wonderful. I need to get your old room cleaned up and I'll make cherry delight—"

"Whoa, whoa. Wait a minute. You're not in any shape to be doing all that."

"Nonsense. I can still make a pie, Jared."

"Okay. Make the pie if you feel like it, but hire someone to do the cleaning—or I won't bring her, Mother. And don't enlist Mari either. She has enough on her hands."

She blew a heavy sigh through the receiver into my ear. "All right. Fine. But you have to at least tell me her name."

"What?" I squeaked. My belly opened up, and my knotted guts poured out onto the floor. At least that's how it felt.

"Her name, Jared. Her name. What is it?" I could envision Cathy Cassidy, ankles crossed, wagging her house-shoed foot impatiently.

I stood up from my desk and paced. "Uhh…" My eye caught the flame of auburn hair outside my office. Words blurted from my mouth before I could connect my brains to them. "Violet. Violet Murphy is her name." *Shit.*

Now I'd done it. My heavenly hot little spitfire of an assistant. Why? Why did she have to be the one?

For nine months, I'd done everything within my power to keep her away. A sardonic chuckle escaped my lips. I'd done everything but make the woman hate me irreparably. That I couldn't bring myself to do. But that wasn't the worst of things I couldn't do when it came to the lovely Ms. Murphy. I couldn't seem to get the redheaded beauty out of my mind. And the more she pushed me away, the more I couldn't stop thinking about her, dreaming about her. Imagining—

"Oh," Mom cried. "I'm so happy and excited. I thought…well, maybe you'd…to make me feel better."

"Why would I do a thing like that, Mom?" I was on the express boat to hell.

"I know. It's silly, but it just seemed like it wasn't real. Like she wasn't real."

Clicks on the keyboard outside my office dispelled that. "Oh. She's real, Mom. You can be sure of that."

A squeal of delight flew through the receiver, piercing my eardrum, reminding me of Lori. What had I been thinking to screw that wench? "Okay. I'm glad you're excited."

"I've been so depressed since yesterday, but this gives me hope, Jared, and hope is something I haven't had a lot of recently."

Jesus Christ. I couldn't imagine a punishment bad enough for what I deserved. What had I done? "I'm glad you're happy, Mom."

"Please say you'll both stay the full two weeks."

"Of course we will." What the hell. I'd come this far. Might as well dig the grave a little deeper.

"You were going to bring her all along, weren't you? To surprise us? Well, I won't tell your sister. It will still be a surprise to her."

"Oh, yes." I sank back into my chair. "It'll definitely be a surprise."

Chapter Three

Violet

Jared didn't typically yell or scream, unlike other bosses within the company. I eyed Maddie, the CEO's assistant, down the hall. Now that I'd had a moment to get some perspective, it was clear: Jared's reaction had been one of fear and frustration, not directly aimed with me. He generally left a wake of flattered women in his path. Dazzled girls who would do his bidding regardless of what he asked. He never left cowering hordes.

But his mother was sick. That much I knew, and I had a feeling things had just gotten worse. I understood worse from my own life.

I sat hesitantly at my desk, listening to the murmured one-sided conversation, waiting for him to finish. After a while the office was silent, and I stepped in.

Jared sat at his desk, his eyes a clouded mass of some emotion I couldn't identify.

I waited near the door in case I had to make a run for it, and said in the most soothing voice I possessed, "Everything all right?"

His eyes flicked up to me. "No. Not much."

My chest warmed. His face was unguarded and bereft. A great urgency to hug him enveloped me, but I sighed instead. "Anything I can do?"

"Yes, as a matter of fact, there is." He held my gaze, his mobile features changing in an instant from vulnerable to calculating and coming into direct focus on me.

I shivered a little. "Sure. What do you need?"

"A two-week fiancée."

"Pardon?" I shook my head so I could hear him correctly.

"A fiancée, a wife-to-be, a bride."

"A...*bride*?"

He nodded once. "Someone beautiful, smart...convincing. For two weeks." His focus was still on me, heating my body, but his look was shrouded again and gave nothing away.

What in the heck did he want with a fiancée, and how was I going to procure one for him? "I suppose I could call a professional matchmaker, but beyond that, I don't even know where to begin to look for one." Bewildered, I sank into the chair in front of his desk.

"I do." He leaned forward, all flexing muscle and intensity.

I shivered again, traitorous heart going *thump, thump.*

"In this room." A sly smile spread over his face, teeth sparkling.

It was a smile meant to disarm and dazzle, and I had to admit some susceptibility. *Some* susceptibility? I inwardly laughed at myself. But then dawning understanding spread over me as his meaning seeped into my brain. *In this room? A fiancée in this room?* The sensation that had caused me to shiver became an electrical current zinging rampantly through my limbs. "Oh, no." I shook my head in horror. "No. No, no, no." I took a reflexive step backward.

He rose from his desk and nodded. "What will it take?"

My arms trembled and my fingers tingled, the blood advancing and retreating in a tide of dread and secret traitorous delight. "I won't do it. Not for a year's salary."

"How about for five?" He advanced closer.

"Five?"

"Five."

That would be nearly half a million dollars. I gulped.

"I'm serious, Vi." His incalculable gaze penetrated mine, and I was lost in it.

I struggled to catch a mental breath and shock my system into a reboot.

But he stood there, hands in his pockets, his face open and vulnerable. "I need you to do this. My mother is dying. They've given her three months to live." He tossed his head back and stared at the ceiling, trying to regain composure.

Tension coiled in my chest and drew me to him. The urge to throw my arms around him nearly engulfed me again. Dang his vulnerability and dang my stupid heart.

"This will be our last family gathering. She wants to see me settled with a happy future, so I told her I had a fiancée."

"You lied to her?"

"It wasn't precisely a lie. It just wasn't the whole truth."

I shot him a skeptical gaze.

"All right. I lied to make her happy, and I can't get out of it." He sighed. "I don't want to get out of it. It made her happy, Vi." He met my gaze again, his eyes glistening. "I want her to be happy and to do that I need you." He stepped closer and took my hand in his.

I need you. How could he need me? Why did he need me? I gently pulled my hand away. He was breaking me down and we both knew it. "I bet you say that to all the girls." Mustering a brave front, I added as much flippancy to my tone as I could scrape together.

It wasn't enough because that brought a grin to his face. "Not anyone. Not ever." But there was something there in his eyes firing deep and beckoning me forward. "Will you help me?"

The plea in his voice undid me. This was how he sucked us all in. And, yes, I was counted in that number. I argued with myself, *I'm not doing this because of his eyes or the vulnerability he just revealed.* No. I was doing this because Jared Cassidy had promised me a boatload of money. Sure, *that* was why I was doing this.

I was pathetic. I sucked in a bracing breath. "All right."

Chapter Four

Violet

"You can't do it, Violet." Lucy Furey, SC Endeavors's in-house counsel paced in one direction.

"This is what he does to all the girls, Vi. That's why they call him Casanova Cassidy." Maddie paced the other.

I sat sunken into a piece of a large leather sectional shaped like an L. A giant eighty-inch flat screen was fixed to the wall in front of me.

Back and forth they went in a crisscross pattern that was making me dizzy. I'd called them here into the media room to get their perspectives. To give me perspective, really.

For the past few days, I'd mulled over the possibility of not going. But our flight to Florida left tomorrow, and I needed to either back out or shut up. "I know this is always what he does. But doesn't that give me a tactical advantage? I won't fall for his line, because I already know it's coming."

Lucy shook her head as if to say, *Poor, pitiful child.* The smartly dressed attorney took a deep breath and caught the gaze of her fiancé, Lucas Luck, SC Endeavors's other in-house counsel. "I'm sorry I didn't tell you this before, Luke." She turned back to face me. "But I have to tell it now."

"Tell me what?" Luke's voice growled as he folded his arms across his chest.

Lucy visibly gulped. I think we all did. Luke was pretty hot when he had his jealousy on. Oh, who was I kidding? The man would be hot standing in an ice storm wearing a bunny costume. He was just that kind of guy.

Lucy bravely continued on. "A couple of years ago, Jared talked me into his bed. We went out after a work party. Some deal I don't even remember. We drank too much wine, and he charmed me into having sex with him."

"You did what!"

We all jerked our heads toward Luke, who was fuming.

He pounded his right fist into the other palm with a loud smack. "I'll kill him."

Lucy smiled. "You know legally you can't do that, honey, but it's so exciting to see you want to."

He looked down in shock at his own clenched fists then scowled at her. "We'll talk about this later."

He stormed out. Lucy stared after him with stars in her eyes.

I cleared my throat.

She shook off the daze and turned back to me. "You can't insulate yourself enough, Violet. He knows all the angles, all the tricks to get you into his trap. When he opens up, it's not for real. You think it is and you open up too."

"So what happened with you two?" Maddie sat down on the short side of the sofa and looked up at Lucy.

"I fell for him. After we'd spent the night in my apartment, I came bouncing into his office the next day to ask what he was doing for lunch."

"Oh no." I dropped my head in my hands, my gut churning. Anyone with a passing acquaintance could see what had happened next.

Maddie shot me an inquisitive glance but Lucy just nodded her head.

She plopped down across from us and fingered a headset on a side table. "Yes. What he was doing for lunch was his assistant on his desk."

I winced and confided, "You never know what's happened in that office. That's why I always keep disinfectant wipes handy."

"Oh, Lucy." Maddie put her arm around the cute woman, who also happened to be a formidable attorney. "That must've been horrible."

She flashed us a self-deprecating smile and nodded. "I'm just glad I found out early on. But you know what? It wasn't that he screwed me one night and twelve hours later had moved on. It was that I had trusted him. I'd believed we'd had a true connection. I believed he'd really opened up to me." She pulled back from Maddie's hug and slapped her palms on her lap. "It could've been worse. And now I have Luke and have never been happier." She frowned and focused on me. "I don't want the same thing to happen to you, Violet."

"Me either," Maddie agreed. "But I also think you should go if you want to. Jared was selected for you by DataMatch, and, let's face it, girls, that program has gotten it right a few times."

"It did for me and Luke. That's certain."

I frowned. "Except for when it matched you with Nathaniel Scorge and Lewis Tate."

Maddie's face clouded into some frustrated emotion. "I don't think DataMatch made a mistake."

"What?" I could hardly keep my jaw from dropping. This was the first time I'd ever heard Maddie voice concerns about her match with Nathaniel Scorge. From the moment she'd found out about the DataMatch test pilot, even during the whole Tate litigation, she'd been steadfast in her love for our CEO and determined not to allow Lewis Tate into her heart. "I thought you wanted Scorge."

"I do," she huffed out, blowing a wisp of her brown hair out of her eyes.

"And I thought that you guys were a sure thing," Lucy stated.

"We were," Maddie blurted out, then heaved a frustrated sigh, and amended, "We are. It's just…Nathaniel wants something I can't give him."

Lucy and I looked at each other. The attorney wore the same confused expression I was sure covered my own face. In unison we asked, "What do you mean?"

Maddie waved us off. "It's nothing and this is supposed to be about Violet, not me. Suffice it to say that DataMatch generally gets it right and we can't discount that. But Jared is still a horn dog, so just be on your guard."

As it seemed that was the end cap to the conversation, I headed back to my desk. I'd already told Jared I'd go to Florida, and I wanted to. Clearly, Lucy and Luke didn't want me to, but Maddie had voted for me to move forward with caution.

If I just had one more opinion. Just one more would be the answer.

No. That wasn't right.

The bottom line was I'd already said I would go and I wanted to. What was I trying to do? Protect my heart? For what? Who exactly did I think I was waiting on? Since that Joe guy in college, I hadn't even been on a date. That had been three years ago. Whether written in the stars or the software, math or mythology, horn dog or hero—I needed this for me.

I picked up the receiver from my desk phone and dialed.

"Hello." The familiar voice tickled my ear.

"Mom, I wanted to let you know what's going on."

"Is everything all right?" Concern laced her words.

"I think so." I took a deep breath and told her about DataMatch and Jared and his reputation and his mother. And finally I told her his plan.

Just like always she never judged and only listened. "And you want to do this?"

"I want to help him. I know what it's like to lose a parent."

Her voice came soft and sweet over the line. "That you do, honey. I just have to wonder if his mother is the only reason he asked and you want to help."

"I also want to see for myself if what is between Jared and me is real."

"I thought so. I've never seen you feel connected with any man outside your movies and romance novels. You've been alone too long. No matter what happens, it's good for you to open up, Violet, and let someone else into your life."

I didn't know why but her words made me want to cry. "I let people in. Leona from college. Gary."

"Gary doesn't count, sweetheart. He's my friend."

"He comes over for Christmas. I see him at holidays."

I could see her chiding look through the phone. "No. It doesn't count. And when was the last time you called Leona?"

The truth was I hadn't talked to my college roommate since I'd graduated and gotten this job. "Well, I have friends here at work."

"Have you gone out to dinner with any of them?"

I didn't want to answer that question for fear of incrimination. "Lunch?"

Ha! "Yes, as a matter of fact, I went out with a group last week for lunch."

"Really. Who went?"

"Well…everyone. It was a company luncheon."

"Mmm-hmm. Like I said. You need to let people in, Violet, even if it hurts. And I won't lie to you: It will hurt sometimes, but you can't live all alone forever. You need people. Your father would never want you to shut yourself off like this."

"So you're saying this trip is more about helping me than Jared?"

"I think that maybe it will be about you helping each other."

Chapter Five

Jared

"Here. Let me get that." I grabbed Violet's bag and lifted it into the overhead bin. My heart thumped. What the hell was wrong with me? My heart hadn't raced like that over a girl since…

You'd think I was a fifteen-year-old on my first date with Alex. Not that Alex would've ever called it a date. Who gives a crap what Alex would've called it?

Violet sat by the window and buckled herself into the plush leather seat. I'd sprung for first class tickets, because I damn well couldn't abide riding in coach. This flight was proving to be stressful enough, and since it was on personal time and I wasn't expensing it, I wouldn't have to listen to Nathaniel bitch about what a waste of money upgrades were. Because as far as I was concerned, first class was worth every penny.

I stuffed my carry-on next to hers and sat in the aisle seat, making a production about getting settled and buckled in because, honest to God, I didn't know what to say or where to start.

She removed the fashionable scarf she wore and twined it in her hands. "Flying isn't my favorite thing."

My breath hitched. She had to be one of the most beautiful women I'd ever seen. Top ten percent at least. "Don't worry. People in first class rarely die."

A strand of auburn hair fell over her blue eyes and she pushed it back with dainty fingers. She wore a sleeveless blouse the color of salmon, and I could see fair skin and a hint of freckles dusting her arms. The same fair skin was modestly revealed at her neck and chest. I couldn't help but wonder if those freckles covered the perfectly formed breasts teasing me from under her shirt.

She rolled those deep-blue Elizabeth Taylor eyes at me. "Gee, thanks. That makes me feel so much better."

My heart tripped over itself, and I felt pissed. Damn. Having sworn off sex until after the trip, I'd gotten little-to-no sleep last night. That by itself was enough to make me antsy. But lying alone in my bed, I couldn't get thoughts of creamy skin and auburn hair from my depraved mind. I hated being alone, which was why I always strove for temporary company. Last night had been torture. I shot a sidelong glance to Violet. I couldn't imagine what these two weeks would be like.

This trip down celibacy lane had been a requirement of Violet's, and I couldn't disagree with her. It wasn't like I could have a fiancée and bring home some strange girl from the beach to bang. I never did women at Mom's anyway. But Violet had not only made me get a new phone number for the trip, she'd made me break it off with the women in Chicago too. That was fine. I didn't care enough about any of them to keep them around anyway, and I could replace them when I got back. But I could already feel my balls filling with the need for release.

"So should we practice?"

I turned my head toward her and narrowed my eyes. Relief was in sight. "Practice what? We're in public right now, not that I'm opposed to some mile-high action, but maybe we should wait until the plane takes off."

Her face flushed with color. "You're disgusting, you know that? I'm talking about going over the details of our story so that we don't get caught in a lie."

"Oh. Right." Our story. Where to begin?

The plane barreled down the runway then lifted.

Violet gasped and grabbed hold of the arms of her seat.

"I know a way to alleviate your fears," I teased in my most seductive voice.

Just as I'd hoped, her usual look of indignation covered her face. "I don't think that will be necessary."

I licked my lips and loved the way her pupils flared. Teasing her was a double-edged sword. Flustering her, making her go all schoolmarm on me, gave me a secret joy I'd never known, but it was skirting disaster.

I'd never met a woman I couldn't forget, walk away from, or leave behind. But I'd known from the moment I met Violet that she was different, and I needed to tread lightly. I'd flirted and even boldly propositioned her, but if she'd ever once taken me up on the offer… Well, I couldn't think about that.

What I did want to concentrate on was helping her, and if I couldn't help her by seducing her, then I'd have to think of something else. "Are you always so afraid of flying?"

She gulped and forced out the words. "Always. That's why I rarely do it." Her breath was shallow and her face paled.

"Why does it frighten you?" I focused my gaze on her, forcing her to look at me.

She blushed and smiled timidly. "I don't know exactly. Maybe subconsciously I feel like I still have a lot of life left to experience, and flying equates death."

The pilot leveled out the plane and the seatbelt sign dinged off. Her grip on the armrest relaxed. I picked up her hand and placed it in mine. "What do you want to experience before you die, Violet?"

She met my gaze boldly. "I want a man who loves me. Someone on whom I can lavish the wealth of treasure stored up in my heart."

My body flushed with instant anxiety.

"I want a husband who will cherish me, who will give me himself body and soul and allow me to give myself. I want a best friend, a lover, a confidant, and a companion who knows me better than anyone."

My heart thundered in my chest. My breath snagged in my throat and sweat beaded on my forehead. I couldn't speak. My damn vocal chords had taken a hiatus with my brain.

But she didn't seem to want me to say anything because she kept talking. "In short, I want what my mother had. A man who loves me more than his own life."

I dropped her hand and folded my arms across my chest. Women told me shit like this all the time. Usually, I smiled and nodded, unaffected, but as Violet spoke emotion spiked inside of me. I saw her vision, and for the first time I could ever remember, I wanted it too.

What was happening to me? I needed to concentrate on the task at hand. "All right. Fine. No need to go crazy sentimental on me."

A small speculative smile curved her lips. "Nope. None at all. So what do we need to do?"

I caught my breath. "You'll be meeting most of my family so let's start there."

Chapter Six

Violet

"Okay, you two, follow me." Cathy Cassidy moved slowly down a short hallway in her small family home.

Our late evening arrival had been met with peals of laughter and squeals of delight by Cathy, Jared's mother; Mari, his older sister; and Marvis, Cathy's nighttime hospice nurse.

Every inch of my skin had burned with the scrutiny of the three women, who had looked at me like I was a cyclops unicorn. No surprise: Anyone who'd known Jared for as long as they had must be in shock over meeting a steady girlfriend. But after the preliminary inspection, I was welcomed with the same warm, open-armed hugs they gave Jared.

He'd squeezed my hand and smiled sweetly—a look so honest, I had to mentally slap myself back to the reality of my situation. Jared was playing a part, and so was I. That was all. I could not let myself ever forget that. If I did, I knew I was doomed.

"You can both sleep in your old room, Jared." Cathy opened the door to a small bedroom.

Sleep in the same room? I gasped then coughed to cover my misstep when all eyes focused on me.

Jared flashed his trademark smile, clearly understanding my shock and taking full advantage. He placed a hand on my back, drawing little circles at my waist with his thumb. The sensation heated my body.

Behind Cathy's back, I clenched my jaw and narrowed my eyes at him. Then I plastered on the daughter-in-law smile I'd been perfecting and stepped into the dark little bedroom.

A wave of nostalgia swept over me in the face of Jenifer Aniston, whose sexy pose was tacked to the wall with mismatched pushpins. A tower of CDs sat in the corner next to a mammoth stereo with speakers that came to my waist. I studied the alphabetical titles that included Jane's Addiction and Janet Jackson. It was a rare peek into Jared Cassidy's youth.

"I'll give you two time to unpack. When you're done, you can have Mari make some coffee to go with that Bundt cake Marvis made." Cathy closed the door behind us with a resounding *click*.

We were alone. Together. In a bedroom. I tried to keep my heart from pounding, but I might have to stop it altogether to do that.

"Don't be getting any ideas, Vi. This isn't *The Proposal,* and you aren't Sandra Bullock. I won't be sleeping on the floor to assuage your honor. I'm sleeping in the bed."

I pursed my lips and crossed my arms over my chest. "They're bunk beds, Jared."

"But you have to be on top." He grinned like a Cheshire cat.

"Yeah, well. You're no Ryan Reynolds, so I'd never expect you to act like a gentleman and give me the bed…at least not without you in it." Actually, he was hotter than Ryan Reynolds, but I'd go to the grave with that info.

Then as a realization hit me, I spun to face him. "Wait. You're telling me you've seen the *The Proposal*?"

"What can I say?" He shrugged. "I dated a girl for a few months who wouldn't have sex unless a romantic comedy was playing." He rested his shoulder against the bunks and crossed one leg over the other.

I leaned toward him, unsure. "I don't believe it."

"What?" He draped one arm across the base of the top bed, looking sexy and mildly insulted. "You don't think I could sit through a romantic comedy to get laid?"

"Seriously? Jared, you could sit through a Russian Parliament session for sex. I just can't believe you dated anyone for a few months."

"Ha, ha. The joke's on you then." He snatched up a pillow and tossed it in my face, plopping me onto the bottom bunk, which bounced as I fell. His brown eyes heated. "Why, Miss Violet, you look positively pluckable sprawled across *my* bed."

"I am not sprawled." I scrambled to my feet, but by the time I'd composed myself with some amount of dignity, he was long gone, to the kitchen probably, where the smell of something so wonderful would pull anyone with a nose.

When I got there, Jared was already at the table with a piece of cake in front of him.

"Come in and sit down, Violet," Mari said as she set a piece of cake in front of an empty chair. "Coffee?"

I nodded, taking a big whiff of the cake. Lemon. Mmm. "Coffee is great."

She placed a steaming mug in front of me and sat next to her mother at the little four-person dining table.

The kitchen's distressed whitewashed cabinets seemed new, as were the countertops and tile. Light-colored wainscoting lined one wall and the bar. I took a deep breath and rotated my shoulders. The room felt cramped, but that may have just been me feeling a little out of place. Actually, the room was warm and homey.

Marvis, who was a sturdy gray-haired woman probably in her mid-sixties, sat at the bar because there wasn't room at the glass table. I leaned back against the cushion of my white wicker chair, taking everything in. This had obviously been their home for a long time, but why hadn't Jared bought her a new house? It wasn't as if he couldn't afford it.

He frowned as if reading my expression. "Because she wouldn't let me. Mom likes things exactly as they've always been."

Cathy swiped playfully at his arm. "That's not true. I let you redo the living room and both bathrooms. And I let you replace all the kitchen appliances."

I glanced around and noticed the stainless steel looked a little misplaced in the country kitchen with its rooster and harvest-apple-cart motif.

"And even that was a trial. Violet, if it hadn't been for our constant nagging, you would have arrived to mauve carpet and dusty-rose wallpaper." Mari laughed. "It was hideously outdated."

"It really wasn't until my daughter, Ava, who was four at the time, told Mom her house smelled like the grocery store." She took a bite of cake.

"How many kids do you have?" I took a taste from my own plate.

"Two. Ava, who is now eight, and Corey, who's four."

I nodded and turned back to Jared's mom.

Cathy was handling the good-natured teasing well. "I would've been content to keep everything as it was, but I let you both have your way."

Mari took a sip of coffee. "Come on, Mom. Tell the truth. You have to admit you love relaxing in that Jacuzzi tub."

I smiled, enjoying their family banter. It showed how close they were. I was close with my mom too. And I couldn't imagine losing her.

Cathy hung her head in defeat. "I do enjoy my soothing soaks." She turned to Jared. "Your Aunt Penny is coming later this week and Julie will follow."

"Are the cousins coming too?" Jared asked. "Do we know how many rooms we need?"

"Six, probably." Cathy took a drink of from her cup. "You two will have to get your talent together."

Jared blinked. "We haven't done that in a while."

"With everybody here, Penny thought it might be fun." Cathy shrugged then focused her gaze on me. "So, Violet, how did you meet Jarry?"

Jarry? I arched my eyebrows and glanced to my right. "Yes, *Jarry*. We should tell her the story of how we met."

His smile was bright but his jaw ticked.

Nervous energy coursed through me. I'd debated back and forth about whether or not to come and play the part. I wondered what I would do if my own mother were dying.

Jared had spent the better part of three hours coaching me on the plane, in the rental car, and in the driveway when we'd arrived. We were supposed to play the consummate couple in love, clearly on our way to the altar. According to Casanova, aka Jarry, he had not yet formally proposed, but we'd talked about marriage and knew the deed was imminent. I still wasn't convinced we could pull it off, but I felt the overwhelming need to try for his mother's sake.

Late last year, the doctors had found a malignant tumor—the bad, fast-moving kind—on her lung. She'd had surgery to remove the mass, but a portion of it was dangerously close to a main artery. The procedure had been tedious and long, and the doctors could not remove all the tumor. She'd followed up with harsh chemo, radiation, and immunotherapy, but nothing had stopped the progression. It had continued to spread throughout the other organs of her body. And then there was nothing more the doctors could do.

Jared and Mari had looked into alternative treatments, but Cathy had refused. Her body had been weakened significantly by the treatments, and she wanted no more. Personally, I couldn't blame her. The treatments sounded just awful.

This two-week vacation was to be their last family gathering. Relatives from all over the country were coming in for the Fourth of July family reunion. Apparently it had been a yearly occurrence when Jared and Mari had been kids, but as they and their cousins had grown up and away, the gatherings had become less frequent.

So to make his mother happy and fulfill her dying wish, Jared had upended his life for two weeks and convinced me to come along for the ride.

He'd gotten a new phone number that only a handful of people had access to, and he'd—temporarily, at least—broken off all ties with his *entourage*.

He was staring at me now, the gleam of deception in his eyes. "Well, let's see. It was at work, wasn't it?"

I knew about spy work and undercover operations from my romantic-suspense fetish. In *Lure: Dangerous Secrets Book Two*, Calvin, an undercover narcotics officer, gets in with a drug runner's daughter, and they have to come up with a cover at a family gathering. Calvin told Jennie, the heroine, the best way to convince someone of a lie is to stick as closely to the truth as possible. I could follow that advice.

So I smiled and said, "Yes. We met at work when we were matched up by the company's new online dating software."

Cathy tilted her head, glancing back and forth between us. "Really? Is this the new program Nathaniel is having so much trouble with?"

"One and the same," Jared agreed hesitantly. "Although I'm not sure if it's the program he has issue with."

Concern clouded his mother's features. "You don't have to share Violet with another man, do you?"

I shuddered. She knew that much about DataMatch? I glanced at Jared, who winked.

"Violet, haven't I told you before how Mom, Mari, and I met the Scorge family? It was when they opened their first hotel here in Palm Beach. Mom was hired on as the first housekeeper, and Mari and I helped her in the laundry room and kept out of sight of the guests. For the most part."

Both Mari and Cathy laughed out loud at that.

Mari set down her coffee mug. The thirty-something woman was as beautiful as Jared was handsome, with the same coloring and complexion. "The way I remember it, little brother, is that I did the work while you sneaked around Mom's housekeeping cart."

"All right. I wasn't as stealthy as I should've been." He turned his attention back to me. "Nathaniel and I used to play when we were kids, and our families became close." The look on his face told me there was more but now wasn't the time.

"I didn't realize. I guess we've never talked about how you met Nathaniel." My cheeks heated. The CEO's given name came out awkwardly, and I knew I would never have the guts to call him that to his face.

Mari arched one dark eyebrow. "Knowing Jarry and his *appetites*, I'm surprised he even lets you talk at all."

"Jarry" threw an arm around my shoulders and slid my chair closer to his. "It's true. In the beginning, we barely talked at all, did we, sweetheart? We barely even got out of bed. But trust me when I tell you that my appetites are nothing compared to Vi's. I could hardly catch my breath before she was at me again."

I felt a sinkhole of humiliation the size of Miami open underneath my chair. My face, my neck, my chest, and even my toenails flushed with horror. "Oh my God. *Jared*, that is not true, and your mother is sitting right there!"

Cathy leaned back in her chair and laughed so hard her eyes watered. She could barely catch her breath. Mari snickered, and even Marvis was chuckling.

I, on the other hand, could not find the humor, but what I would've preferred to find was Jared's face with my fist. I could've killed the man.

I only read about sex. I never talked about it, and I certainly never did it, either. In fact, I'd only had sex once in my life, and that had been with the wrong guy—the way wrong guy. I'd decided then and there, lying on my back and naked from the waist down, that sex with the wrong guy wasn't for me. I was determined to wait for the right guy. I'd been waiting a long time. I glared at Jared. Clearly, I would be waiting longer.

I speared a piece of cake with my fork and imagined it was my Casanova. My face had to be ten different shades of plum. As a redhead, I didn't blush demurely. Oh no. With my fair skin, my flushes were ugly and obvious. Blotchy would be an apt description.

Jared nuzzled his nose in my ear and whispered, "Sorry, Vi. I couldn't resist."

I glanced down at the fork in my hand and willed myself not to stab him with it.

When the laughter died down, Cathy took a tissue and dried her eyes. She looked sheepishly at me. "Don't worry, honey. We all know Jared can be an ass sometimes." A racking cough tore at her throat, and she gasped for air.

Mari hurried to the corner and rolled a small tank of oxygen to her mother. She placed the mask carefully over Cathy's nose. "Here, take a few breaths. Jarry's got you all riled up." Mari's tone was soft and teasing. It held no real censure, just concern.

Cathy inhaled and immediately stopped coughing.

"Don't blame me." Jared held out his hands in a plea of innocence that, based on the look of the women, would fall on deaf ears, or at least ears that knew better than to believe the denial. "I couldn't help it. The look on Vi's face."

All three women chuckled in response, Cathy's chuckle drowned in the clear plastic respirator.

I glared at him as I took my last swig of coffee, letting him know this wasn't finished.

Jared flashed an easy smile, but his gaze flicked over his mom's equipment.

Mari stood protectively by the ailing woman's side. "It's late, Mom. You've been up a long time. We should get you into bed."

Cathy nodded. She pulled the mask free with one hand and patted my arm with the other. "You two have had a long flight and should get some sleep too. We'll talk in the morning."

I squeezed her hand where it rested on my arm. "I look forward to it."

Mari and Marvis helped Cathy from her seat. I hadn't realized how truly feeble she was. The excitement of seeing her son had obviously given her a surge of energy she didn't normally possess. It was painful to watch the women slowly help her to her room.

Jared and I quickly finished our cake and coffee and headed down the hall behind them.

Chapter Seven

Violet

As soon as the door closed, I turned on Jared. "What in the world would make you humiliate me in front of your family like that?"

He flinched a little. "I was wondering if I'd ever get to see that redheaded temper."

Anger speared through my veins. Growling softly, I stepped into his space, coming face to face with him, annoyance and aggravation swirling. Our noses nearly touched, and a strange excitement radiated off him as much as it wafted from me. The sensation stunned. I blinked in confusion, trying to gauge Jared's response.

"My hair color has nothing to do with my anger. I do not appreciate being the brunt of your little joke." I refocused, remembering why I was riled. "I have never been so mortified in all my life."

"I don't know what you're so upset about." His dark eyes swam with heat, his lips pressed together tightly.

"That figures." Up close I could see every nuance of his features, but I couldn't tell if he was suppressing the urge to laugh or scream. I didn't care. Actually, I did, but I couldn't let myself care. "Do you want me to go out there and tell your mother what we're doing? What you're doing?" I moved my face in closer and glared. "Do you?"

His gaze darkened as it focused on my puckered lips, his eyes almost closing because of how close we were. "You know you're unbearably sexy when you're angry."

The husky pant of his words whispered against my prickling skin. Another sensation more dangerous than anger flooded me. My heart thumped in triple time. I reluctantly lifted my chin. His body surged with passion that rolled over me in waves. He was going to pull me closer. Worse, he was going to kiss me. I could see it all, right there in the darkened intent of his brown eyes, as if this were a romantic movie. I inhaled sharply, arousal and awareness snaking through my body. Fear of what he was about to do shivered down me, fear of what I wanted him to do. *No.*

My palms flattened on his chest, the feel of his solid frame shocking me as I shoved. I took a leap back, trying to catch my breath and regain control.

He stood perfectly still, his face clear of expression. Then a smile stole over his lips. The storm of sensation had passed. At least for him. And he chuckled as if it were all some big joke.

Rekindled anger seethed inside me again. How could he just turn his desire off and on like a light? I stared unbelieving for a short moment. Anger continued to burn me, but now with the additional sting of humiliation.

"I can't do this." I shook my head, realizing for the first time how true it was. "I don't want to, Jar—"

"I wanted to make her laugh." His words broke mine off, though they were soft. His face was sober and honest. He slid his hands into his jean pockets, looking so sexy and incredibly vulnerable. "I'm sorry, Vi. I just wanted to make her laugh."

My throat tightened, and just like that, my anger drained away.

"I was always the one who knew how to make her laugh. Everyone said so. Even when I was little."

I stood there trying to catch my breath, trying to keep from caring. I wanted to hug him, kiss him, and kill him for making me feel this way.

His gaze grew wistful. "After my father left, she didn't smile or laugh for weeks—except when I teased her or Mari." He looked up at me as if realizing I was there in the middle of his memory. "I couldn't do much for them after my father left. I was young, too young. But I could always make them laugh. That was what I could do."

The helpless look on his face squeezed my heart. I groaned in utter frustration. I didn't know if he was playing me or not, but either way, he was forgiven. I put a gentle hand on his arm. "I'm sorry, Jared. So sorry. Cathy seems like a wonderful, amazing lady, and she certainly doesn't deserve this."

His muscles twitched under my fingers, and his dark brown gaze locked with mine.

"None of you do." I heaved a heavy sigh, unable to comprehend what this loss would mean to them.

We stood there like that for a long moment. Finally, I cleared my throat. "So, I get the top bunk?" I asked, raising my eyebrows and looking at the bed, which was covered in some ancient, ugly, geometric-patterned comforter.

A faint smile played over his lips and he nodded.

"What did your mom mean about our 'talent'?"

Jared shrugged. "It's sort of a tradition. We always have a talent show along with the family reunion."

"You mean like a performance?"

"Exactly."

"But surely, I won't be expected to…"

"Everybody under the age of sixty is expected to…" He waved his hand and scrutinized my body as if assessing my merit for family-reunion talent shows. "Winning is a source of great Cassidy family pride."

"I don't know, Jared. I'm not particularly talented."

"I find that had to believe." Something shifted deep in his eyes, and then he was playful again. "So, do you prefer getting wet at night or in the morning?" His voice purred, thick with insinuation.

Still overwhelmed by the talent-show bombshell, I blinked. My hands trembled, and I fisted them at my sides. "I'm not sure I understand." Or that I wanted to.

He chuckled again. "I mean the shower. Do you prefer morning or evening?"

I swallowed down my stupidity. "Regardless of how obscure, have you ever met an innuendo you didn't do?"

"No." A big deep laugh rumbled from his chest. "Not too many."

"I didn't think so." His audacity made me smile. He was a man created for seduction, and one more than capable of using his talents. "But to answer your real question, I shower at night. I like being clean when I go to bed." I slapped a palm to my forehead, realizing as I said the words exactly what I'd stepped into.

And right on cue, he said, "Not me. I prefer to be as dirty as possible in bed."

I could hear him laughing as I made my way to the bathroom. I was sure everyone could.

I took a shower, letting the steady stream of steamy water beat out the tension in my back.

Why was I here? What was I hoping to accomplish? At first, I'd thought it was the money. Then I thought it was because it would please a dying woman. But now, alone in the bathroom stripped of all pretenses, I had to be honest with myself. I desired him, wanted him, but even deeper than that, I cared for him. No wonder I'd been so mortified by his suggestion that I was insatiable for him. It might've been funny to Cathy and Mari, but it was too close to the truth.

"Violet Rosalyn Murphy, you are doomed. Doomed, I tell you." I closed my eyes, positive of the hopelessness in my situation.

There was no getting around it. I could prevaricate all I wanted, but the truth of the situation was that I already cared too much about him, and I had come on this god-forsaken mission to find him. Find the real Jared beyond all the smoke and mirrors, the flirtations and flings. I wanted to find the man I knew was buried under there. The one I'd rarely seen, but knew, by faith, was there. Mom was right, and apparently DataMatch had been too. In him, I'd found a kindred spirit, someone to relate to.

"This place holds the key." I'd hoped it would. Now, I even knew part of the problem: his father. Same as me.

From the little I'd gathered, the man had left them when Jared was small and had never returned—or even tried to contact them. I knew better than anyone how the loss of a father could affect a child.

I'd been only seven when my own father had left. Except my father hadn't left by choice. Knowing Jared's father left of his own free will, I imagined the hurt and anger he felt was worse than mine, and that betrayal was part of why he had trouble trusting anyone. But that that wasn't the whole story.

I huffed at myself. "And when you find out all this enlightening information, what are you going to do with it? Do you think he's going to open his heart and allow you in, just like that?"

No. In fact, I feared the opposite was true. I knew getting beyond the walls was just the first step, and the most dangerous, because he would do anything to protect himself once he felt completely vulnerable.

I turned off the faucet and grabbed a towel.

Chapter Eight

Jared

The shower stopped. I yanked a T-shirt over my head, trying not to imagine Violet's wet skin, or wet anything. Damn if that thought hadn't made cotton out of my throat.

The vision of a towel sliding over the expanse of that fair skin played in my mind. I shook it off, dropped to the floor in front of my old stereo, and popped in a CD.

This arrangement was only for two weeks. I could go two weeks without a woman—especially that woman. I'd done it before.

Hadn't I? At some point in my virginal past. Jesus. Did I even have a virginal past? I cranked the tunes up a little, but not too much. Didn't want to wake the house like in the old days.

See, I had plenty of other things to occupy my mind beside the plump backside of Violet Murphy. Too many other things.

Mom's coloring was damn near gray. She looked like she had effing elephant skin. What the chemo had done to her was heinous. I wanted to puke or beat the crap out of something. Maybe both.

I scrubbed my face hard, trying to remove the image. Three to six months and she'd be gone. Three to six fucking months. My chest tightened to the point of explosion, but I held back the roar that wanted to burst free. What the hell kind of timetable was that? I had women in my life every day, but there wasn't one of I couldn't do without, except that one. Even Mari I could get along without if I had to.

Mom didn't deserve this mess. She'd kept us together after Dad left. Kept us in this house. She'd always been the one to hold it all intact, which is why she never would let me buy her a new one. This house was the symbol of her accomplishment. It was her trophy to show the world she could do it all on her own.

The awareness of this place, the feel and smell of it, was enough to drive me mad. I hated nostalgia almost as much as I hated cancer. The past wasn't something to dwell on—or even think about if I could keep from it. But I couldn't keep from it when I was in this place.

Maybe I should go back to contemplating Violet. Was the hair between her legs the sexy shade of auburn that shimmered on her head and drove me wild? Or was she a dye-job?

"Nah. I'd bet my left ball it's all the same color."

"What's all the same color?"

I turned to catch Violet staring and flashed her an unrepentant smile, trying to recover. "You're lucky I decided not to wear my usual attire."

"Which is what?" Her tone aimed for flippant.

She could do sassy better than any woman I'd ever met—and I'd met a few. I licked my lips. "I think you already know the answer to that." I scanned her sleek form. Even clothed in the soccer-mom pajamas, she made my body tighten. "Mmm. You look...*comfortable*."

She lifted her chin. "I am."

Janet Jackson played softly. I turned back to the music, letting it take me away.

Violet was a beauty. I didn't have to date her to know we'd be explosive bed partners. But a girl like Violet expected more than just bed partners. And *more* was something I was neither inclined to nor capable of giving. So I strove to make that fact evident every time I saw her, while still keeping the offer of hot, sweaty sex on the table. Or the desk, or the bed. Hell, wherever she'd agree to it—and eventually she would. They all did.

"I used to love her music."

"Yeah. Me too." I opened the CD case, memories flooding back to me. What the hell. Couldn't stop them anyway.

The wooden ladder creaked as Violet climbed up and crawled onto the bunk. "Will this thing hold me?"

"Yes. It's been through rigorous testing."

"I can imagine."

"Can you?" A heavy sigh escaped her, and I grinned despite myself. "Be careful. I can hear your eye roll from down here."

"Who's this blonde girl?"

"What blonde girl?" I flipped off the stereo and stood.

"Look how skinny you were. There are pictures taped to the wall up here. They're all of you and a blonde girl."

The hair on my arms stood up and the skin on the back of my neck prickled. "Forgot those were there." There were at least five, if not six. I should've thrown then away. "That's Alex." I tapped the CD case against my leg, trying to sound casual or anything other than what I felt, which was a stiff kick in the balls.

"Did she die?" Violet asked softly.

A laugh slipped from my lips, but there was nothing funny about it. "Worse: She married a preacher."

"Why is that a fate worse than death?"

I returned the CD to its case. The outside was cracked. I knew how the thing felt. "Because it wasn't me."

"Oh."

There was plenty expressed in that one word. I shot a gaze up to the top bunk, encountered the piercing crystal blue of Violet's, and darted a look back to my hands. "Does that surprise you?"

"I don't know. Did you ask her to marry you?" Her voice was soft but not filled with dewy-eyed sympathy. She was just curious, as if there was some grand riddle she was trying to puzzle out.

It allowed me freedom. I didn't think this woman was interested in me for a romantic relationship any more than I was with her. That was the only excuse I could provide for how I was opening up my history with Alex. "Never got the chance."

"But you wanted to…"

Vi's hesitation forced a small smile from me. I'd never told the story to anyone. Of course, no one had ever known to ask, except Nathaniel, and he didn't have to. He'd been here along with Mom and Mari that summer.

Maybe I should shut the door on the subject, but now that it was open, I didn't care to. "Yes. I wanted to."

"What happened?"

I flipped off the light and fell back onto the bottom bunk. The whole structure shook and creaked.

Vi squealed. I grinned.

"This thing is sturdy. It'll withstand a lot. Trust me."

"I'm just afraid previous abuse and years of misuse has caused the wood to weaken."

"Hmm… I hadn't thought of that. It could've."

"I'm sleeping on the floor." The frame swayed and thumped the wall as she tried to get out.

I chuckled. "It's fine, Violet. You're completely safe. From the bed, that is. Besides, if it does break, I should be the one to worry.

You would crush me under a weight of wood and your deliciously plump backside."

She squawked in protest. "I don't have a plump behind. Delicious or otherwise."

"Prove it."

"Why don't you just tell me about Alex?"

The darkness closed in on me. Would this be the last time I ever slept in this bed? In this house? The thought sent a jolt of pain through my chest that closed around my heart like a length of barbed wire. A thin band of moonlight streamed into the room from underneath the curtains. I focused on the light and my story. "What do you want to know?"

"Everything."

I couldn't stifle the laugh. The excitement that laced the word was palpable. "Women love for a man to talk."

"Just to talk? No. But to talk about something meaningful? Yes." She rustled in the bunk as if to get comfortable.

"Don't settle in too much. The story isn't that long or that entertaining."

"I'll be the judge of that. So, *go on*."

"All right, all right. Don't soak your panties." I leaned back against the headboard. "Alexis was my next-door neighbor and best friend from the time she and her family moved in when I was seven years old until I graduated high school. She was the only female friend I've ever had."

"Except me."

I paused and thought. I considered how Violet and I had this heavy attraction/loathing for each other. And on occasion she bailed me out with irate female companions. And called on my help for big things like when Lewis Tate threatened to sue us and Nathaniel threatened to shoot him. Or when Maddie and Nathaniel were arguing so loud a crowd was gathering outside his office. "Yes. I suppose I count you as a friend."

A little squeal of delight came from above, but not enough to deter her from her recon mission. That's what this was, her female way of gathering information to somehow use against me at a later date.

"And you loved her?"

I groaned. "You're gonna make me say it, aren't you?"

"Of course. I may get to be the only girl alive who's ever heard those words cross your lips."

"And, just so we're clear, this will be the last time they do."

"Fine."

"Yes, I loved her."

I heard a soft gasp then a recovery. "But you didn't tell her?"

"I shouldn't have had to tell her. She should've known. At least asked or given me some warning before she started dating that idiot Burns."

"Wait." The bed hissed and banged the wall like she had shot up in it. "So you're saying, you've never told her?"

"No. I never told her. So now you know another one of my dark secrets, Miss Murphy. What are you going to do with it?"

The silence was deafening. The air conditioner kicked in. Blood pumped thick and wary through my veins. I couldn't suppress the fear that I'd made a mistake by telling her. It was almost as if, once opened, the door to that part of myself couldn't be shut. I felt naked and exposed to her in a way I never had with a woman. Needed to lighten the mood. Needed to find new defenses. "So you tell me a secret. It's only fair."

As if relieved to have the subject changed, she said, "What do you want to know?"

I wasn't sure if I liked the idea that she hadn't been riveted by my revelation. Actually, it pissed me off. I'd just flayed open a piece of my soul and she wanted to move on without even a bark of protest. My blood bubbled in a slow stew. You know what they say about paybacks. I aimed my sight for the one hot button of hers I knew. "So, blossom, tell me: What's the best sex you've ever had?"

"That's a shocker of a question, coming from you. If I'd had one guess as to what you'd ask, I'd have won some money."

"You wouldn't get your money until you answered the damn question." I sounded pissy. I took a deep breath. *Calm down, Cassidy.* This was just a little getting-to-know-you talk before stripping off clothes and going at it like animals. That's all.

There was a long pause.

"Violet?"

A soft sigh escaped her. She whispered, "I've never had good sex."

The way she said the words seemed like she was blaming herself. "That's a shame. You know I'd be happy to assist you with that dilemma?"

"I'm aware."

She wasn't aware. I hadn't even been aware of the depth of my desire until she said the words. Something coiled deep inside my gut. My cock stirred. I closed my eyes and pushed images of amazing sex with Violet out of my mind. Okay. You got me. Maybe I didn't push them completely out of my mind but to the back of my mind. The far back. On the left side, in a dim, candle-lit corner, with a firm bed and soft sheets and fair skin shimmering in the light of the flame—

"Shit."

"What is it?"

"Nothing." Nothing but a throbbing hard-on and two weeks of deprivation for the poor bastard. "So what's been wrong with all the sex you've had? Tell Dr. Jared the problem. Maybe I could give these guys some pointers."

"There's no plural. Only singular."

"Huh?" Plural? Singular? What the hell was she talking about? A threesome?

"One guy, not many guys." She cleared her throat. "I've only had sex with one guy."

"Oh. I see. You had a long-time boyfriend."

Somehow the thought of Violet with a boyfriend didn't sit well in my chest. My chest? Shit. The day—or night—I started having thoughts in my chest, they might as well cut off my balls and rip up my man card. I was beginning to think this whole opening-up conversation was a disaster. My teeth clenched. So she'd had a boyfriend—

"No. I didn't have a boyfriend. I had sex."

I blinked and contemplated. *"Once?"* I hadn't meant for my voice to crack, but the thought of her...anyone...getting to be her age without sex more than once was unbelievable. A woman as gorgeous as Violet only having been with one guy one time? What was wrong with the male species? I was fast losing my faith in the ability of man to procreate. "You're shitting me."

"Only once. And trust me, if it had been as bad for you the first time, you might not have considered doing it again either."

"Damn." I blew out the word with a serious force of sympathy.

"I know, right? Anyway, I don't like to talk about it. So tell me: What are your favorite romantic comedies?"

How bad would sex have to be for me to never want to do it again? I couldn't compute the possibility. Now I felt guilty, but I wasn't sure what I felt guilty about. For having great sex or having so much of it? To make her feel better and to play her little get-to-know-you chick game, I tossed out the first movie that came to mind. "*Pretty Woman.*"

"Of course you would like that one."

I narrowed my eyes and glared up at her even though I knew she couldn't see. "What's that supposed to mean? It's a perfectly good movie in the appropriate genre."

"Anything with a prostitute would be your pick."

"I've never paid for sex." I'd never had to.

"That I believe."

Sex was something that came naturally. I didn't grow into my body until the summer I graduated. That summer Alex got engaged. I also got engaged…in carnal activities in the back of movie theaters, in the backseat of Mom's old Sentra, on the beach, the ball field, and the bathroom of the local McDonalds… *Focus, Cassidy.* "What about you? What are your favorite romantic comedies?"

"There are so many. I don't even know where to start. Well, I would say the one that means the most to me is *The Goodbye Girl.*"

"Richard Dreyfus? Geez, you're reaching there, Murphy."

"I know. It's an oldie."

"Although Richard Dreyfus is in one of my all-time favorite movies."

"*Close Encounters?*"

"No."

"*Mr. Holland's Opus?*"

"No."

Silence.

"Oh. I know. *Jaws.*"

"No." I settled down into my bed, sniffing the familiar scent of bulk-buy detergent that Mom got from the hotel vendor. The smell sent me back to the days of my youth when Alex had been allowed in my room. She'd take the top bunk and we'd talk like this for hours. "Don't hurt yourself."

"I give up."

"*What About Bob?*"

"What about him?"

"That's the movie: *What About Bob?*"

"*What About Bob?* is your favorite movie?"

"It's funny. Forget it." I turned to my side and watched a sliver of moonlight slowly track across the carpet. "Anyway, tell me: Why is *Goodbye Girl* your favorite romantic comedy?"

"Actually, I liked the movie okay, but it's the song that I truly love."

"Why? You weren't even born when that song came out. Hell, I wasn't even born."

"It was the movie that my dad took my mom to on their first date. It reminds me of my father, and of the kind of man I want to find for myself."

"Huh." Her words struck a chord in me. That craving of so long ago to be that kind of man for one special girl. The kind of man who loved his wife and took care of his kids. But that jet had left the hanger years ago. "What does your father do?"

"He died when I was seven."

Chapter Nine

Violet

Strange Buddhist-monastery music filled my dreams. I sucked in a long breath and stretched my hands over my head.

The hum of human voices, the reverberation of a gong, and something that sounded like one of the monks had dropped the silverware tray harmonized to make a genuine sound.

My eyes flew open, and I peered over the edge of the bunk. My vision was a bit foggy because I hadn't removed my contacts the night before.

Bright sunshine streaked in from the window. The curtains had been pulled back to reveal a row of small beach houses on the other side of the road, and beyond that, a beach and water.

This was a sight I hadn't seen last night when we'd arrived. It had been too dark. But I had felt the balmy breeze and smelled the sea. And I'd heard the distant crashing of waves. This morning it was all illuminated—including tall, dark, and sexy.

Jared was bent at an impossible angle in front of the speakers, his firm abdominals in my direct line of vision, and I didn't need contacts to see lean lines of a well-formed six-pack. I licked my parched lips and suppressed a crazy urge to lick him instead. His eyes were closed, and he was in an obviously meditative state with one arm and one leg extended in opposite directions—an advanced yoga move, I knew. The monks continued to sing their buzzing song.

"What in the hell?" I whispered.

Jared's eyes opened, and he peeked at me from underneath his bare torso. "Good morning."

He twisted to the other side. The muscles of his smooth, olive-skinned back flexed with effort. I realized I was licking my lips again and panting a little. His muscles bunched and rippled as he brought his leg and arm back to the ground then stood, but not before he gave me a perfect view of his firm backside. On purpose, no doubt.

Oh God. I sat up and pulled the covers to my chest, feeling a bit vulnerable and a lot turned on. "Good morning." My voice was a husky squeak.

He turned his body to face the beds and tilted his head up. "Thought I might need a little meditative peace of mind today."

"Do you do yoga often?"

"Every once in a while." He flipped off the Tibetan chamber music. "Have you tried it?"

"Once. I got a free class with one of my college roommates. That was enough to tell me I wasn't built for it."

"Nonsense. Anyone can do yoga."

"But I'm not anyone."

"Come here and I'll teach you a simple move that you can start with." He propped his hands on his hips, waiting for me to move. The elastic waistband of his pajama pants sat low on his hips and a sheen of sweat made his body shine in the sun. I felt like I should kneel at his feet, but knowing him, he probably got that reaction all the time. His shoulders appeared broader than they did hidden under his shirt and the heavy sprinkling of dark hair over his well-defined pecs screamed, *I'm a man and a god.*

I gulped down my pounding pulse and forced my gaze to remain above the Mendoza line. Geez. He was beautiful.

"Trust me, Vi. I used to teach yoga." He smiled and I nearly fell out of the bed.

My best bet for safety was on the ground, so I climbed down. But I still stood near the bunks.

"Here. Let me show you." Jared took my hand and pulled me to the center of the room. His skin was warm, but his fingers were lean and strong. "Do you know table pose?"

I shook my head. Imagining something far different than what he was suggesting—although, knowing Jared, maybe not.

"Gently lower yourself onto all fours."

That just didn't sound right. I flashed him a skeptical glare.

"Don't look at me like that. I'm trying to help. You look like a knot of nerves." He roughly massaged my shoulders. "On your knees."

"I bet you say that to all the girls."

He chuckled. "Now who's using innuendo? Come on. No more dawdling."

I lowered to my knees, trying to forget how sexy he was when he was barking orders.

He stepped behind me. "Palms on the floor, Murphy, shoulder width apart."

I obeyed, feeling a little silly with my round parts protruding in different directions.

"Take a deep breath, then slowly release." He placed a palm on my lower back and a tingle rippled through the parts all around that area. "Tighten you abdominals so your lower back doesn't sag."

"I do not have a saggy back." My voice sounded threaded, but I did as instructed, breathing in and out in long deep motions.

"In. And out." His voice turned soft with a mesmerizing cadence.

I continued to breathe, focusing on my abs and the warm hand on my lower back.

"Now stretch your arms out in front of you, slowly breathing your forehead to the floor." He slid his palm up my back to my shoulder, showing me the range of movement. Waves of pleasure washed over me. "In. And out."

My forehead touched the carpet. Long-tensed muscles began to loosen. Stiff joints from a nervous night in a strange place began to give way. Joints and tendons unwound and desire flowed like rain. I wanted Jared to touch me all over and to never stop.

"That's right. Just allow yourself to relax." His voice got even quieter. "In. And out."

The confusing jumble of thoughts and voices in my head dimmed.

"Hear only the sound of your breath." Jared's voice was barely a whisper now. "Feel only the dance of your body, beating, pulsing."

I concentrated on the steady beat of my pulse and the slow, rhythmic inhale and exhale. My mind drifted in weightless wonder. I floated in a tranquil sea. I imagined swimming with Jared in pools of water warmed by the sun.

In. And out.

Ebb and flow.

Back and forth…

"Do you want some breakfast?"

His voice startled me out of the trance. I opened my eyes and blinked, my body coming back to consciousness. Slowly rising, I noticed Jared's hair was wet and a towel was draped around his neck. "You took a shower?"

"Yep. And shaved. You were out for a while." He pulled me up from the floor. "Josie has breakfast made."

"Josie?" I stretched my stiff legs and rotated my neck.

"Mom's daytime hospice nurse. She normally just fixes meals for Mom, but she's made us breakfast as a treat. Bacon, egg, and cheese burritos made with her homemade flour tortillas."

That got me up and awake. "I love homemade tortillas." My mouth began to water as I gathered my clothes.

Jared headed for the door. "Me too. So hurry up or I'll eat yours."

I could hear him traipsing down the hall to the kitchen. My body hummed, rejuvenated and alive. Maybe there really was something to that yoga stuff.

I quickly dressed and headed to the kitchen.

Jared was at the table, already gobbling down one of two good-sized breakfast burritos.

Cathy sat on the other side, finishing a cup of coffee. She smiled when I walked in. "Hey there, blossom. How did you sleep?"

I smiled at her endearment. That was what Jared had called me too. "Slept good, but Jared showed me a new move this morning that really relaxed me." I sighed appreciatively.

Jared froze, his burrito suspended midway to his mouth. Horror struck me as my X-rated comment reverberated through the room. Heat swept my chest and face like a brush fire.

"Yoga. A yoga move."

After last night, that clarification hadn't helped much.

Cathy's eyes sparkled with mischief. Now I knew where her son got it.

A little Hispanic woman set a plate in front of me.

Grateful to be distracted, I said, "Thank you. I'm Violet. You must be Josie." I held out my hand.

The sweet-faced woman smiled and took my hand in both of hers. "*Sí.* Josie."

It was evident from her response that she understood English but perhaps didn't speak it too well. Based on the smell coming from my breakfast and Jared's stuffed mouth, she could cook. I took a bite. The burrito was a perfect combination of fresh vegetables, melted cheese, and eggs. I sighed.

Cathy watched but didn't eat. "I was hoping you could help me go through some things in the sewing room today."

I glanced up from my plate. She was looking at me, and had obviously addressed the comment to me. Not Jared. I gulped down the bite of burrito just a shade before chewing it long enough, and dotted my mouth with a paper napkin. "Me? You want me to help you?"

"If you don't mind." She fiddled with a ruffle on her dressing gown as if she was embarrassed for asking. "You see, Jared is going to run to town for a few things we'll need for the party. I've asked him to put up a canopy in the backyard for shade and to set up a few picnic tables underneath."

"Don't forget I need to replace the privacy boards around the bathhouse." A little bit of egg spewed from his full mouth as he spoke.

She nodded and took another swig of coffee. "The guests don't come until next week, but I'd like to clear out the sewing room before that."

"I'd love to help you." I wanted to put her at ease. "I'm honored you asked."

"Great. We'll get started right after breakfast." A brilliant smile lit the frail woman's face, and I could see so much of Jared there. The sight squeezed my heart.

"You may not think that when you see the room." Jared pushed the empty plate away and leaned back in his chair. "It's a mess."

Cathy folded her hands primly in her lap. "It's not a mess. It just has a lot of stuff in there. Stuff I need to sort through."

I shot Jared a quelling look. "Every woman needs a place to keep her stuff, Jared. You wouldn't understand." I waved my hand dismissively. "You go to Home Depot and stay outside today."

"All right. All right. I know when I'm not wanted"—his gaze flared and heated—"and when I am."

My cheeks burned again. He'd noticed me ogling him this morning. I shrugged. No sense blushing over spilt desire. So I boldly eyed him in his board shorts and sleeveless T-shirt. What wasn't there to want when it came to Jared…well, except for the obvious?

Chapter Ten

Violet

"It looks like we need another Hefty bag. Here are some more clothes." I grabbed an armful of hanging garments and lifted them from the back of the closet. Dust flew in every direction.

When Jared had said the room was a mess, he hadn't been lying. This room was crammed to maximum capacity with the gathered stuff of a lifetime. There were trinkets and baubles, old appliances, and pictures. There were boxes of keepsakes, and lots and lots of old clothes and linens. I plopped the load of clothes on the bed and reached for a box of plastic bags.

"You might as well grab two, blossom. This box is filled with old beach towels that need to be given away too."

"At least that's everything in the closet." I shook out the folded bag and snapped it open.

It had taken the better part of two hours to clear a path and empty the closet. I didn't want Cathy moving too much, so I'd plopped her into an old upholstered rocker and told her she needed to supervise. I'd lifted, carried, emptied, and transferred items into one of four piles: the trash pile, the giveaway pile, the Mari pile, and the Jared pile. There were three full bags of trash already, two full bags and three boxes to give away, and a few items of sentimental value that had been distributed between the two kids.

After I emptied Cathy's box of towels, I stood next to the pile of hanging clothes, holding up each item and either discarding it or keeping it at her word. "I'll save these hangers. Mari may need them." I swiped a stream of dusty sweat before it could trickle into my eye.

Cathy nodded. "That's a good idea. When my kids were young, I remember never having too many."

"Meez Cathy. You *medicina*." Josie stood in the doorway holding a small tray.

"Come on in, Josie. If you can find a walkway." Cathy laughed.

I tossed down the blouse I'd been folding and helped clear a path for the nurse. She set the tray on the bed and handed me a glass of freshly squeezed lemonade before giving Cathy her pills and another glass of the icy treat.

"I have lunsh in *una hora.*"

I wondered what kind of meal she would prepare. My mouth was already watering I was so hungry. The last time I'd worked this hard was when Mom had decided she wanted to have a garage sale. I groaned at the memory.

"What are we having, Josie?" Cathy asked after she downed her pills.

"Sheiken and rice."

"I love sheiken," I said with a smile.

The little woman chuckled.

I swiped the glass across my forehead, letting the condensation cool my sweaty brow, then used the napkin Josie handed me to wipe away the dampness. A layer of dirt and grime came with it.

"Josie, I think Cathy might need her oxygen. It's dusty in here. Not good for her breathing."

"Oh. Don't go making a fuss." Cathy's cheeks heated.

She clearly hated being a bother and hated being on oxygen. Even though the doctor had ordered she be on it all the time, she refused to wear her breathing device except at night. But in this musty room, her face had turned red and she'd struggled to get enough breath.

Josie studied her then turned to me. "*Sí.* Meez Cathy need her *oxígeno.*"

"I'm going to need a bath after this." I fanned my shirt, feeling like I'd tattled on my friend.

Josie had quietly departed and quickly returned. She placed the breathing tubes over Cathy's head and turned on the machine. Cathy's body instantly relaxed and color returned to her cheeks.

"I guess I need to keep it on. I just hate it. I hate it all."

"Me too," I murmured, pushing back the sadness. I was here to help her, not go all maudlin. I straightened my back and began working again.

Cathy was now watching me intently, a shimmer of emotion in her eyes. "It's been a long time since this room has been cleared out. You didn't know you were going to have to work when you agreed to come, did you?"

"It's okay." I put another pair of slacks in the giveaway bag. "I really don't mind. In fact, I'm enjoying myself. This is something my own mother would have me do." I picked up my lemonade and took a sip, then set the glass back down. "But I do have to wonder why you asked me—a complete stranger. Isn't this something Mari would want to help with? I mean, all this stuff has significance to you and her. I feel a little like I'm intruding."

Cathy patted the gold and blue flowered scarf on her head as if unsure it was still in place. "Going through this room would've been too hard for her. It's a very real reminder of the inevitable. This way, we'll pack up the memories, and she can go through them when she's ready."

My throat clogged with emotion. Though I'd known Cathy only a few hours, I could already see that her every thought, her every care, was for her kids. I folded a polished cotton dress with shoulder pads the size of my head and cleared my throat. "This is an old one."

"I think that one's actually older than Jared." Cathy smiled sadly and met my gaze. "I asked you to help me, blossom, because I wanted to get to know you, and for you to get to know me. Going through the stuff in this room is a crash course on our lives, a way for you to puzzle out who we are, so that after I'm gone, you'll know you belong."

A stab of guilt jolted me. I closed my eyes, bracing against the pain. "I'm so sorry, Cathy." She wouldn't understand the true extent of my words, but I meant them all the same.

"There's nothing to be sorry for." She reached over and patted my arm. "Can I tell you a story?"

I stopped folding the jeans I had in my grip and covered her hand with mine. "Sure."

"When I met Jared and Mari's father, Alejandro, he was the most handsome man I'd ever seen in my life. Now, mind you, I wasn't as worn as I am today and could hold my own in the looks department."

That I could believe. Her skin was laced with wrinkles and her hazel-green eyes lined with years of hard work, but it was evident to me she had been exceptionally beautiful as a girl.

"But no man had ever overwhelmed me like Alejandro. It was love at first sight. He was only nineteen and I only seventeen. We met during Christmas of my senior year in high school. He'd fled from his home in Nicaragua after the assassination of his friend and mentor in 1979, and had traveled via Cuba to Miami, where I lived with my mother and father."

"From the moment we met, we were inseparable, but my parents were firmly against our relationship." She reached for the next piece of clothing, a sweater, and began to help me fold. "After a few months of sneaking around, I found out I was pregnant with Mari. Alejandro was elated. He had applied for a job here in Palm Springs and insisted I come with him. By that time, I only had a few months left of high school. Knowing my parents would never consent, I packed a few belongings, left a note, and went with him in the middle of the night."

"You ran off with your lover? How exciting." I reached for another hanger.

"It was. For a time. Alejandro and I both worked at the hotel. He in maintenance and me in housekeeping. It was the only job I could find without a diploma. Alejandro didn't even need a green card. They never asked in those days.

"The first two years were hard, but they were like heaven because we were together. Then Jared was born in 1985 and our family was complete. It felt like nothing could ever tear us apart. We worked the same schedule. We never fought, and we were happy."

I felt the doom in her words. "But there was something."

"Yes. Nicaragua."

"Nicaragua?" I wasn't sure I understood.

"You see, the mentor who had died left a widow. By 1987, the woman had revived her husband's following and urged all his supporters back home, including Alejandro."

I had stopped folding and sank onto the bed to hear the rest.

"He left in early 1988 to return home and meet with her. We both knew it would be dangerous. For one, he'd have to sneak across the border both ways, and then, even if he could do it, that part of the world was in political chaos. There was no guarantee he'd make it back.

"But in my heart, I knew it was something he had to do, so I encouraged him to go. He took two weeks' vacation from the hotel and set out, saying he'd contact me when he got there. He was gone for nearly three months, and I never heard from him." She smoothed the wrinkles from her cotton dress. "I struggled to make ends meet, using some of our savings to supplement his missing income. The hotel eventually terminated him, and I feared the worst.

"Finally, one night in early summer, he showed up. I was beside myself with joy and anger. Nothing appeared to be wrong with him, but he was different, distant from the moment he walked through the door. He had moved on to a place where neither I nor the kids could reach him."

"Oh my God. Do you think he found someone else?"

She shook her head. "No. He found his country, his cause. He'd become bitter. He blamed the United States—and, by extension, us—for the political turmoil in his country. You may be too young to remember, but the American scandal in that region was world news back in those days. It was a black mark against us."

"Then what happened?"

"He left the next day. Packed his stuff, which I now believe was the true reason for his return, and never turned back. The wife of his mentor eventually became the president of the country—the first woman president in the Americas—and he became one of her top advisors. I found out some years later that he had married and had children."

"You two never married?"

"I know. It was foolish of me. That should've been a red flag that something wasn't quite right." She brushed a few stray tears from her eyes. "Ah, well. I wasn't the first woman to have her heart broken by a handsome man claiming to love her, and I won't be the last."

"But he didn't even care about his kids? What kind of man does that?"

"I think he may have wanted to keep the kids, but he knew he wouldn't get them from me without a fight. And I think, ultimately, they would've been a source of embarrassment for him. I don't think anyone in Nicaragua, including his family, knows about me or the children."

I wrapped my arm around her. She hugged my waist.

"I'm so sorry." The weight of her broken heart sat for a brief moment on my shoulders, and I wondered how she went on all those years.

"He left me with the most precious possessions I've ever had: my kids. Even knowing what I know today, I'd live it all again to have them just as they are. And to have him just as he was, even for that short time." She released me and pulled back to look in my face. "But you don't have to worry about that, sweet Violet. When Jared gives his heart, it's for good and it's forever."

My chest tightened with pangs of more remorse. This woman had been through so much. And here I was deceiving her on her deathbed. Even if Jared felt it was for her own good, it didn't feel like that to me. It felt like a dirty trick. I squeezed my eyes shut in agony.

"You stop that right now." Her voice held a stern warning. "There is absolutely nothing to feel guilty about."

My eyes flew open. I started to say something, but she gave me "the stare," the one all mothers know how to give. My own mother was an expert at it. So was Jared's.

"You think I don't know that Jared is trying to pull one over on me, young lady?"

The hair on the back of my neck stood. "W-what?"

"Don't give me that. I know he thinks he's convinced me you two are dating, but any fool can see you aren't. Yet."

"Oh no." My shoulders sagged. "I'm so sorry. He just wanted you—"

"Blossom, you don't have to tell me why he's doing it. I know, and that's why I'm letting him get away with it…for now. It keeps his mind occupied. He needs to keep busy or he gets into trouble."

"Can't argue with that."

"But what I want to know is why you're doing this."

"W-well…uhh…you see—"

"He's paying you, I'd imagine. But don't say it's the money, because I'm a better judge of people than that. Tell me the truth."

I blew out a long sigh. "My father died when I was seven. I know what it's like to lose someone you care about. I wanted to be here for Jared, and I thought I could bring you some happiness too."

She studied me with her hazel eyes. "Yes. I can see that's part of the reason, but I think you care about Jared more than you're letting on."

It seemed all my secrets were doomed to exposure with this woman. "But you know I can't let myself do that. I shouldn't. He's not a safe bet. He's going to break my heart, Cathy."

"Maybe not." Her voice was hopeful.

"But you don't know what he's like with women." It sounded like a whine.

She tilted her head and arched her eyebrows, if she'd had any eyebrows. "Oh, I know better than you give me credit for. Let me ask you something: Do you trust me and my wisdom? Do you trust my knowledge of my son?"

"Yes. I guess." The words came out shaky and a little tentative.

"Then do me a favor. Will you?"

"I don't know." A tremble of fear shook me. "I'll try."

"Open yourself up to the possibility of Jared. Just while you're here in my house. Let him show you who he is...with us. Then make up your mind if you want him or not."

"But what if he doesn't want me?"

She tilted her head forward, giving me "the stare" again. "I thought you were brighter than that."

"Hey."

A smile brightened her serious face. "Nathaniel told me Jared refused to date you, even though this fancy computer program picked you as his perfect match."

Wow. She did know a lot more than she let on. Jared would not be happy when he found out Scorge had revealed his secrets. "That's true."

"Why do you think that is?"

"Excuse me?"

"Why was Jared so adamant about not dating you, when he dates practically anything with a skirt?"

"Because...I'm not his type? He's not attracted to me?"

She snorted in a loud and unladylike fashion, and I thought the breathing tubes were going to go flying. "If you can't tell that boy is crazy about you, I'm not sure what I can do to convince you. Everything about you calls to him like a siren's song. Maybe he doesn't let you see it, but when you're not looking..." She shook her head as if she'd revealed too much. "He didn't push you away because he doesn't feel a connection to you, Violet. He pushed you away because he so strongly does."

I sat there blinking at her like a brain-dead cucumber.

"Lunsh is ready, Meez Cathy."

Chapter Eleven

Violet

Jared sauntered in the kitchen door, letting the screen slam closed behind him. Dark hair dusted his forearms. His sleeveless tee was damp with sweat and streaked with black, but the skin underneath was smooth and muscled. His hair was slicked back, and his face and hands were clean from where he'd obviously washed up before coming in.

My heart pattered and my senses strained toward him. Standing there in the light of the sun-drenched kitchen, he looked and smelled dirtier, sweatier, and a thousand times sexier than I could've ever imagined. *Gulp.*

"Got the privacy wall fixed, and the toilet flushes without flooding Mr. Pensky's lawn." He bent and kissed Cathy on the cheek, then took a seat beside her. "So what have you two been up to?"

My cheeks heated to the temperature of habanera salsa. "Nothing much. Still working on clearing out the sewing room."

"My ears were burning. Were you talking about me?" He flashed a grin as he picked up the casserole of chicken and rice and brought it to his plate.

"Oh yes," I said matter-of-factly. "Your mother was showing me all of your school photos. And those cute bare-bottomed baby pictures she has stored."

His hand froze in mid-scoop. He cast a scandalized look at his mother. "Say it isn't true."

Cathy shrugged, obviously forcing back a laugh. "Are you finished with that dish yet?" She pointed to the food still in his hands. "It is customary to allow the ladies at the table first service."

He looked down and paled at realizing his rude error. "Shit, Mom. I'm sorry."

"Watch your language." She dabbed her mouth with a napkin even though she hadn't taken a bite.

I ducked my head and clamped my own napkin over my mouth to keep from laughing out loud. Poor guy was having a hard time.

After seeing that picture of that lanky high school boy, I'd figured he might feel a little self-conscious about photos from his youth. Clearly, I'd thought right. I suppressed a slight twinge of guilt. After what he'd done to me last night, a little payback wasn't unjustified.

We all ate far too much at lunch, but it tasted so good. Afterward, Jared thanked Josie and headed back outside. Cathy and I got back to work in the sewing room, which had been Mari's room growing up.

"After we finish sorting the last of these clothes, all we'll need to do is go through the two picture boxes."

I hadn't lied to Jared about Cathy showing me bare-bottomed pictures of him. I'd seen a few, but once we got the stuff sorted, threw out the trash, and hauled the giveaway piles to the front door, she said we'd sit down in the living room and sort all the pictures between the kids and Cathy's two sisters, Penny and Julie, both of whom were scheduled to arrive with their extended families early next week.

I grabbed one of the last remaining hangers, this one holding an old gray cardigan.

"Keep that one." Cathy pointed to the sweater.

I arched my eyebrows.

"It was my father's. He wore it or one like it nearly every day of his life."

"Was he a fan of Mister Rogers?"

She took it when I handed it to her. Her face became wistful and her eyes teary. She'd told me that after Alejandro had left, she'd reconciled with her family. They had tried to reconnect with her before, but she'd never been open to it. Cathy seemed to believe that her love for Alejandro, and his for her, was a passion so intense no other relationship was sustainable while it still burned. I wasn't sure I agreed, but who was I to contradict.

I reached for the next item and stopped. "What have we here?"

A shimmering dress in the palest of champagne pink lay on the pile. It was covered in clear plastic wrap from the cleaners.

Cathy chuckled and watched me expectantly. "See for yourself."

I glanced from her back to the dress. After gently removing the cover, I held it out to inspect. The neck was scooped and the skirt full with a fluffy petticoat underneath and a thin layer of chiffon over the skirt. It was familiar somehow. Subtle floral beading ringed a graduating drop waist. "It's beautiful." Clearly in a fifties style. "Was it your mother's?"

"No. It was always mine." The sweater dropped forgotten in her lap as she reach out and let the chiffon slide through her fingers. "I want you to try it on. But you need the shoes."

"Me?"

"In the far top left of my closet there is a silver shoebox. Bring it to me, please."

It was a pleasant command, and I wasn't about to argue. I hurried down the short hall into the last room—the only one in the house I hadn't entered. The shock of a hospital bed sat front and center. Other furniture had been pushed aside to make room. I stared at the glaring reminder that Cathy's life was rapidly coming to a close.

"Did you find it?" Cathy's weak voice echoed.

Crap. I scanned the room and headed for the closet. The top shelf was cluttered with more stuff, but just as she'd said, a silver shoebox sat underneath a mile of others. After scanning the room for a stool and pulling over a somewhat-sturdy-looking, straight-backed chair, I stepped up and wriggled the box free from its confines without anything toppling in the process. Professional cat burglar might be an option if SC Endeavors didn't work out.

I slid the chair back in place, turned off the lights, and headed back to Cathy.

Her hands reached for the box before I could even cross the threshold. She opened the lid, tossing it aside, and pulled out a velvet bag. The contents jingled. She let out a shaky breath.

"What is it?" I peered over her shoulder as she opened it.

Two shiny rings fell into her hand. "They were my wedding rings."

"But I thought you weren't married."

"Not officially. But everyone who knew us believed we were. Alejandro saved up for months to buy them for me before Mari was born so that I wouldn't feel uncomfortable about going to the hospital as an unmarried woman." She smiled sadly, then put the rings and the memory aside. "So these are the matching shoes. What size do you wear?"

"Seven."

"Perfect fit. I knew they would be. And you wear a size six dress?"

I nodded. "You have a good eye."

"I sure do. And that's why I want you to try this on."

"But I'm all sweaty—"

"Fine. Put those last two things in the bag, and we're done in here. Go shower and try on the dress."

"But…" I frowned. "You are really very good with the mom stare."

"Yes. You can imagine with Jared for a son, I had ample opportunity to perfect it. And you're no match for me, so get."

"All right. All right." I stuffed the remaining clothes into the bag and set it at the door.

Then I hustled into the bathroom to take a quick shower and try on the dress.

Chapter Twelve

Jared

The surf thundered behind me, the wind blowing in from the sea. I stood up and glanced around the old yard. It looked the same as it had years ago. Not much had changed. The shrubs had grown up and unruly and the palm trees had sprouted, but the house was still the same white wood with dove-gray accents.

I wiped sweat from my eyes and got sawdust in them. "Shit." I dropped the hammer and picked up the hose to rinse them out.

Violet had thrown me off balance last night in more ways than one. I'd had no idea her dad died. Jesus. What a fuck-up that question had been. But even worse was how I'd nearly had to shackle myself to the bottom bunk to keep from grabbing her from the top bunk and making love to her until we were both sore and satisfied. Hell, with the way I felt, that might've taken a week. My lower regions ached like the devil.

But it wasn't all physical, and that scared the shit out of me. I was starting to feel something for this girl, and I sure as hell couldn't let that happen. No way. No day.

I held the hose to my mouth and drank, then swiped away the excess and turned off the hydrant. I needed to keep my cool or that little spitfire was gonna have more Jared Cassidy than she could handle.

If I could seduce her, get into that tight, slick—

"Jared," Mom yelled out the back door. "Need your help."

I blinked and adjusted my shorts. I was aching again. I followed the sound of Mom's voice, though I couldn't see much past the back door. Inside, my eyes failed further from being in the sun. I grabbed a couple of paper towels. "What do you need?"

"We need the trash taken out and these bags loaded into Mari's car."

My sister sat at the kitchen table with a Coke. She looked up at me, then scanned down my body, honing in on my barely retreating erection just like she used to when we were kids.

Shit. I propped my hands on my hips, wearing my arousal like a badge of honor and daring her to say something. I refused to blush like a fifteen-year-old.

A bit of her teeth showed in a sinister smile. "Looks like you should be nailing something—or was the wood not hard enough?"

"Ha, ha. Shouldn't you be at work? Is it quitting time already?"

Bored with the game, she stood from the table. "Yeah. I've got to get the kids from daycare, but figured I'd drop the clothes off at Goodwill first."

"Where's Vi?"

"She's taking a shower. She'll be out in a minute."

Mom still had her oxygen on.

"All right. Let me get the trash first."

I toted bags, bins, and boxes to Mari's minivan until sweat ran in rivers down my back. I came in the front door, letting the screen bang me in the ass. "That was the last of them."

Mari and Mom were gathered around each other and hadn't noticed my entrance.

"It fits you perfectly."

"You're stunning. Are you sure you can't do better than my brother?"

Mom stepped back to reveal Violet decked out in some gorgeous dress. I blinked, realization dawning. "Holy shit. The *Dirty Dancing* dress."

"Watch your language," Mom warned me. "What do you think? She looks great in it, doesn't she?"

Violet gasped and looked down at herself as if she'd just noticed she was miraculously dressed to kill. She slapped her thigh. "That's where I've seen this dress."

Did she look great? Jesus. I could have used a few more expletives but decided against it. "She looks amazing."

"You should take her out," Mari so subtly mentioned. "Tomorrow night is the White Party at Rumbass."

Thoughts of the heat, the beat, and sweet, sweaty bodies pressed together made me smile and ache in a good way. Rumbass was *the* Latin dance club in West Palm Beach. I hadn't been there in years. "Maybe I will. But for now I've got to finish setting up the backyard for the reunion and talent show."

The talent show. I clapped my hands together. The girls jumped. "This is it! We've got our talent, blossom. We'll do 'The Time of My Life.'"

"You mean the dirty dancing from the movie?"

"Well, I'll modify it. You dance, right?"

"Uhh…not very well."

"Maybe you just haven't found the right partner." I captured her gaze. Ever since last night when she'd told me she'd had sex only once, my body had burned and my mind had spun out of control with visions of righting that unforgiveable wrong. What kind of a dickass couldn't make proper love to a woman like Vi? That was not a mistake I intended to make.

"I don't know." Her cheeks heated, and I knew we were on the same page.

God, yes, I wanted to sink into that.

"Jared's a great dancer, Vi. He and I used to dance in local competitions together. Anyone can follow Jared's lead. He's a strong partner." She perused down my body with a surveying eye.

"That doesn't surprise me."

"Come on, blossom. It'll be fun. You remember that scene in the movie, right?" I flashed her a grin, hoping it would do the trick.

"Of course. I'm just surprised you do."

"Jared loves romance," Cathy offered. "He watches all the romantic comedies with me."

Jesus God! *"Mom."*

"Does he really?" A sly smile formed on Violet's face. I was busted. "He did mention he enjoys romantic movies."

I scratched the back of my neck and looked away. "Yeah. Well…now you know for sure."

"I guess I do."

I wasn't giving up. This was the perfect talent for Vi and me. It would be her introduction into the family. It was also the perfect way to romance her into my bed. "So let's do it. We'll practice tomorrow night."

"We might need more practice than that," she said, "if you don't fancy being completely humiliated in front of your family."

I snatched up her hand, grabbed her around the waist, and twirled her, stopping before I hit the fireplace. "We might." I leaned in and touched our noses. "And we might not."

Her chest rose and fell. The room was silent, Mom and Mari watching, I was sure. It didn't matter who was watching. I wanted this woman. It was starting to scare me how much. I could be convincing, that was my strength, but I was struggling to hide just how much her answer meant, and not just for the seduction. This was more than that. Violet was more than that.

"So, what do you say?" I swayed back and forth, rocking my flexed thigh between her legs.

Her eyes fluttered back in her head. She swallowed loudly. "Ahh…okay."

Mari squealed.

Mom clapped and said, "I know you'll be great."

Violet met my gaze, face flushed and out of breath. She pushed back. "You're getting my costume dirty, Johnny Castle."

"I know. Where do you think they got the title?"

Chapter Thirteen

Violet

Instead of wearing the *Dirty Dancing* dress to Rumbass, I elected to go with a white halter top and tight-fitting capri pants.

Jared parked his mom's little Mazda SUV three streets over and we walked to the front of the bar. I knew it was the club's front not because of the blazing neon signs blinking like noonday, but because of the United Center-sized crowd waiting to get in.

The line of white-clad people stretched down the block and out of sight. This was going to take forever, if we even got in at all. But Jared walked right past the line, some of whom became haters, and straight up to a guy at the door.

He spewed out a few words in Spanish to the bouncer, fist bumped the guy, then man-hugged him, and we were allowed in. Jared turned back to me. He grabbed my hand and screamed toward my ear, "Stay close. I don't want to lose you in here."

I barely heard him, but scanning the tight crowd I had to agree. If I let go of Jared's hand, it might be hours before I found him again.

To say the bar was packed didn't even begin to describe it. The room itself was dark and foggy, but bright lights flashed through mist and smoke. Loud Latin music pounded and drummed. Jared squeezed me between two bunched-up couples and placed me in front with his arms protectively around me. Still we swayed and jostled with the throng of people.

I'd once seen my Great-Aunt Gladys, my mother's aunt, put on a pair of support pantyhose two sizes too small. I remember watching the fat rolls shift from one side of her body to the other as she inched the things up. As a girl, that sight had scarred me for life. This experience was similar. Only this time Jared and I were the fat roll being squished and squeezed on every side until we were sandwiched together so tightly, I could feel a bulge forming against my backside.

Jared growled in my ear, "Quit wiggling your ass."

I growled back, "You think I'm doing it on purpose?" But I knew he couldn't hear me. I couldn't even hear myself.

Jared scooted us into a slight opening at the bar and screamed our drink order at the bartender.

Two creamy drinks were placed in front of us. I yanked one up and took a sip. Sweet creamy flavor tingled on my tongue. It was like an alcoholic milkshake. "What is this?" I pointed at my drink so even though he couldn't hear me he knew what I was asking.

He leaned over and said in my ear, "Dulce de leche."

"You're kidding, right? *Guys and Dolls?*"

He grinned, so I knew he'd read my lips. He leaned in again. "The Bacardi flavoring acts as a preservative."

I sucked down the drink and picked up his, just to be in keeping with the movie. After I finished both drinks, Jared planted me in front again and slowly pushed us forward onto what might've been the dance floor, but that was a technicality. People were dancing everywhere: around the bar, on the second level, in the back. Everywhere I looked the crowd was in motion.

Jared spun me around and caught my waist as a new song began to play. A cute Latin number. "Bésame." He sang along as he led me in a short swift dance that kept repeating with the song.

Surprisingly, I easily followed the steps and realized that what Mari said was true. Jared was a great dance partner. The longer the song progressed, the more comfortable and confident I began to feel. Sensing my enjoyment, he let me find my own moves in certain spans of the song. As the lyrics began again, he twirled me out and pulled me back in. I landed hard against his chest. My back bent and he leaned over and placed a soft kiss on my lips as the music faded.

His eyes met mine. My heart pounded.

The next song began with a chi chi Cuban piano beat. *Badamp pa bamp, badamp pa bamp.* His thigh flexed, which, I then realized, was firmly planted between my legs. *Badamp pa bamp.* A gasp slipped from my mouth, the sensation shocking me this time as much as it had the first time in his mother's house yesterday. He slowly brought me up and banded an arm around my waist. His hard body smelled of sea salt, sweat, and something unidentifiable that made all the hair on the back of my neck quiver. Muscled planes rippled under my fingers as I wantonly skimmed over his chest. His hips and thighs rhythmically pressed against mine, as his hand splayed over my lower back. The beat of the music dictated his moves, but it seemed everything about the motion was meant to arouse.

Jared sang, translating the lyrics to English, "You're the one, my love. You're the one. The one that I want."

He'd obviously not written the words, or even orchestrated the playing of the song, but why had he felt the need to translate them?

My body shivered and the thought was lost. With each flex of his thigh, the spot between my legs tightened and throbbed. He continued to move with unrelenting purpose. My breaths began to come in pants, and a sheen of sweat covered my surging body. My head spun. I pressed against him, angling my body, giving myself the most pleasure.

"When you're in motion you seem not to care—"

I caught his gaze. It locked onto mine and seared me. The truth of what he was doing rocketed through me. Dear God. He was purposely, systematically bringing me to climax right here on the dance floor. And I was so far gone, I didn't care. I threw my head back. He lowered his lips to my neck. His thigh flexed and hips twisted. Small mewling sounds spilled from me, but no one could hear. I widened my stance and rode him to the increased rhythm of the music. I'd lost all reason. All decency. Faster and faster. My world narrowed to him and me. To the music and the chasm of ache between my legs.

His tongue touched my pulse point. The song hit one final crescendo, and I shattered. A moan tore from my lips, lost in the lights, the fog, and beat. My body pulsed, contracted, and released, and then finally slowed. I collapsed against him.

The song ended.

Another began. This one slower.

I wasn't sure I could stand, let alone dance. Jared held me up, holding me tight and simply swaying. I leaned in and breathed deeply. Sanity slowly returned and mortification set in. Had what just happened really happened? No. No. How was something like that even possible? I'd read hundreds of romance novels, but never had I read anything like what I'd just experienced.

The swirling lights and loud music lent a surreal air to the place, and the drinks I'd had continued to buzz inside me. My body floated in some post-orgasmic high.

Jared pulled back to meet my gaze. My cheeks heated and I couldn't look up at him. But he lifted my chin anyway and pressed his aroused body against my hip. No mockery flickered in his gaze.

Only satisfaction—and not even the smug male kind—which was crazy considering I could feel how wholly unsatisfied he really was.

We danced like that for more than an hour. Sometimes fast and others more slowly. Sweat ran down my back and my front. We'd sat for a short time at the bar and drank water, then went right back to dancing. I couldn't remember ever having so much fun with a guy, or even a girl for that matter. Not at a club.

During a momentary lag between songs, he asked, "You ready?"

I scanned the club, which had only seemed to get more crowded and wild as the night progressed. Several girls had removed their tops and were dancing in their not-too-covering bras. I was certain one couple in the corner was having sex—the real kind. I glanced back at Jared and nodded. "Yes."

He led us outside. The breeze chilled my damp skin, and my ears felt like they were stuffed with cotton. We walked to the car in silence, and he opened my door.

I wasn't sure how to define what happened. Was it sex? Did it matter that we were both fully clothed and in the presence of a thousand people? And I certainly wasn't sure how to define my feelings.

When we reached the house, he turned to me. "Feel like a stroll on the beach?"

"Sure." I slipped my shoes off and left them in the backyard. "Looks like we're ready for the party." I pointed to the canopy and a temporary platform Jared had built that afternoon.

"Aunt Penny and her kids will be here in a few days, and trust me when I tell you, there will be no peace and quiet until they leave."

"Rowdy?" I took the hand Jared offered as we climbed down the six wooden steps to the beach.

"That's putting it mildly."

The tide was rolling in. The surf pounded farther up the beach than it had that afternoon when I'd sat with Cathy under an umbrella, both of us reading.

The soft crash and pull soothed my aching ears, and my sore feet sighed in appreciation when they dove into the cool sand.

Jared, who'd also removed his shoes, watched me wiggle my toes and said, "That's why I always come to the beach after a night of clubbing."

"And here I would've thought it was to have sex with some girl you picked up."

"Maybe that too. But I don't need to do that with you."

"Oh God, Jared." I groaned. A wave of humiliation washed over me like the surf.

"Violet."

"I know. I know, and I'm so embarrassed."

"Violet."

I huffed out a sigh and glanced up at him.

"That wasn't what I was talking about."

"Oh." I hung my head, searching for a sinkhole I could casually walk into and never be heard from again.

"But since we're on the subject..."

"We're not. Just forget I said anything. Did anything. Had anything."

A laugh burst from him. "Stop it. You're killing me." He dropped my hand and doubled over.

"Glad you can find humor in this." My statement held a note of censure but a small smile crept over my lips. His laughing had caused my shoulders to relax and my gut to unclench.

"It was just an orgasm, Violet. Nothing more." He shot me a sidelong glance. "And from the look and sound of it, a pretty damn good one too."

"Great. I didn't think anyone could hear me."

"Just me." His gaze was assessing. "There's no shame in taking pleasure where it's freely given."

My body relaxed even more, but I frowned and slapped his arm. Changing the subject might be a good idea, but I didn't want to lose the intimacy we'd gained, beginning that first night here and then tonight. "Have you...uhmm...done that before?"

"Once or twice." Taking my hand again, he walked us through the thin surf at the far edge of the incoming waves.

I studied our entwined fingers, his dark and strong, mine light and delicate. "Why did you tonight?"

He peered down at our feet in the sand. A breeze blew dark locks from his face. "Because I wanted to, and because I thought you might need it."

Needed it? Lord, yes, I needed it, but I was no charity case. "It was a pity...fuck? Dry hump? I don't even know what to call *that*."

My cheeks heated again and tension filled my limbs. What had I done? With my boss? God, oh, God.

He stopped at the beach's edge and pulled me down to the dry sand. "It wasn't a 'pity' anything." He took our hands and placed them in his lap, forcing me to lean closer. "Listen, Vi. I don't think anything. I wanted you, and I wanted to give you pleasure. It seemed like that's what you wanted too."

"It was." My heart thundered.

"Then forget about it."

"Easy for you to say," I muttered.

"No, blossom. It's not easy for me." He took my hand and rubbed it against his impressively solid erection. "Does that feel easy to you?" Frustration and desire laced his voice. "I've been like that damn near since I met you."

"Wow. I think that's way longer than four hours." I pulled my hand away, my cheeks melting off my face. "You should maybe go to the hospital."

He chuckled, easing the tension of the moment. "Sometimes I think I should. But if you only knew how much I want to make love to you right now…"

I frowned. "Is that supposed to make me give in and let you have your way?"

"Would it work?" A boyish grin spread over his face.

"No."

"Didn't think so." He pulled me between his legs, my back tucked against his chest, his chin on my shoulder with arms wrapped around me from behind and both of us looking out at the dark ocean. "Then I guess we'll just have to enjoy other things."

I couldn't remember ever feeling so comforted, appreciated, and safe. The waves rolled in over the shore that stretched as far in either direction as I could see. Not a soul roamed the sand. Only us. The last two people in the world, at least that's how it felt. It was the most romantic moment of my life.

Then I had to ruin it all by doing something stupid. I spoke.

"I didn't realize you grew up without a dad too."

Being held so close, I felt every muscle in his body tense. "What of it?"

The words were cold and harsh, coming from a wall that was just beyond the charming exterior he displayed to the rest of the world. The charm wasn't the real Jared any more than this wall was. That I knew. I had to find a way in. A way to get to the man inside. "It's not easy growing up without a father. Believe me, I know."

"Yeah. I'm sorry about your dad. That must have been hard."

His shoulders relaxed around mine a bit, and I knew I was walking the right path. It was just a path I'd never chosen to take before now. I knew that in order to have a family and a life like my parents, it was inevitable. I'd never been able to jump…until now. "I found a way to cope. I lived in my books. First it was the Chronicles of Narnia and then Garth Nix's books. During my senior year in high school, I found Jane Austen, and that was my entrée into romance, where I've been stuck ever since."

His breathing evened but he didn't speak. I wasn't sure if he understood what I was telling him. The haze of dissipating drunkenness and the sleepy safety of the moment spurred me on to tell what I'd never told.

"I have no friends, Jared. I never let myself get close enough. I knew Maddie from school, but only in passing, and she's currently the closest thing to a friend I have. My college roommate, Leona, has tried to stay in touch, but I haven't returned her call. That was two months ago, and she hasn't called back. Other than my mother, I am alone."

"That's hard to believe, blossom. You've been nothing but open with me."

"That's what I'm trying to tell you, Jared." I plopped my hands in the sand and turned to look at him over my shoulder. "I'm not usually like this, but with you I feel…open…a connection."

Jared's arms tightened around me and he kissed my hair. No one had done that since Dad died. Mom always kissed my cheek or forehead, but Dad had always kissed the top of my head. Jared's eyes churned with deep emotion. He had to sense the truth of my words.

"That guy in college I had sex with—I barely remember his name. Leona decided that I need to prime the pump before I could find the real stuff. So we found him in a bar off campus. When I say it was awful, I mean it. For him and me. After that, I closed myself off to any kind of relationship. Don't you see? That's what you do too. We're the same."

He tensed again. "I don't see how we're the same, Violet. My dad left me because he didn't want me. Yours left you because he died. It's not anywhere near the same thing."

"But we both close ourselves off from people. You use your groupies and I use my novels."

"Violet, I don't *use* my groupies. We share mutual pleasure without the ties of commitment. The life I live is the life I want. It has nothing to do with my father."

His voice wasn't angry, just resolute. The wall was up and it wasn't coming down tonight. Maybe it never would. I had no choice but to accept what he said, even though I knew he was wrong. "If you say so."

"I say so."

Humiliation bubbled up in my chest. I'd just shared my most intimate detail and was rejected. "Well, thanks for listening to me and my sob story."

He turned me sideways in his lap and tilted my chin up so he could stare into my eyes. "You're no sob story, Violet Murphy." His voice was a whisper filled with wonder, and I realized how so many could be taken in. It was impossible to resist. "You're the strongest, sassiest, sweetest woman I know, aside from my mother. And hang-ups over the past aside, I count you as one of my friends. My close friends."

"So where do we go after…tonight and what happened? It was good, by the way."

He smiled. There was that smug male satisfaction. I knew it was there somewhere.

Then his face sobered. "Vi, I don't expect anything in return for what happened tonight. I wanted you to know how desirable you are, and how great it can be…with the right guy."

"You don't think you could be the right guy?" I asked, bold stupidity welling up again. Someone needed to remind me not to drink the Bacardi.

"Not a chance." He stood and pulled me to my feet. "But there are moments when I wish to God I were."

After dusting off the clinging sand, I took his hand again, because I really liked the feel of it in mine. No war was going to be won tonight, and even though he'd declared the matter closed, I couldn't help but feel it wasn't. I swung our arms out and spun us toward the house. "Let's go to bed."

His faced opened like a little boy on Christmas morning, and in a teasing tone he asked, "To bed?"

I pursed my lips. "To sleep, Casanova."

The emotion in his eyes shuttered. "To sleep. Right. To sleep."

Chapter Fourteen

Violet

"Jared Michael, put me down. I can make it on my own." His mom was kicking out her feet and wiggling in protest.

We were on our way another day at the beach, Jared carrying Cathy across the street and down the steps to where a spread blanket and picnic lunch awaited.

Squawking the whole time, Cathy finally said in disgust, "You'll throw your back out."

He just chuckled and kept walking with me close behind pushing her oxygen tank over the sand. He plopped her down in a lounge chair and offered her a glass of lemonade. The scoundrel wasn't even winded.

I covertly eyed his bare chest, taking note of the flexing biceps and jokingly added, "I wish there was someone to carry me."

Jared spun on his heels, quirked a dark sexy eyebrow at me, and said, "I think I can accommodate that request."

I recognized that look. It was trouble in the making. I started to back up. "Oh no. I was just—"

He scooped me up like a hawk with a field mouse—and I use that analogy because I actually squeaked like a field mouse—then marched down to the beach and into the water.

"Jared, stop. I don't want to get in," I pleaded with him.

His brown eyes were hooded by lids with lashes so long and dark they couldn't be real. "Then why did you wear this sexy swim suit? Is it just to taunt me?" He grinned and tightened his hold. "I don't take taunting well. I think this fear of the ocean has gone on long enough.

"I'm not afraid of the water." And that was true. Partially. Even though my tone held a note of defensiveness. "I'm just not used to it."

"You've barely dipped your toes in the whole time we've been here." He kept walking, and the water kept getting deeper.

Waves sloshed over his calves. I looked down, a little apprehension fluttering inside my chest. "Maybe I don't want to get wet."

Another eyebrow quirk. "That has not been my experience when it comes to you, blossom."

My entire body turned a nice cooked-lobster shade of crimson. I could see the blotchy patches forming on my alabaster abs revealed by my why-did-I wear-it bikini. My heart thundered, but it wasn't only embarrassment. Waves of excitement crashed over me and a restless tension settled in my belly. My body was amazingly and securely cradled in his arms. No guy I'd ever known had teased me like this. Played with me in or out of the water. I couldn't help the smile spreading over my lips but I tried to sound firm. "Jared, put me down."

He waded farther out and a wave lapped at my bottom. We were waist deep. "Are you sure you want me to drop you here?"

I could hear Cathy's laughter and knew I was done for. "Jared Cassidy, so help me, if you dunk me in this ocean—"

He dropped my feet, which splashed into the surf. I screamed and threw my arms around his neck and my legs around his waist, clinging to him like a spider monkey.

His arms went tight around me, his face even with mine and very close. "Now that's what I'm talking about." He grabbed my bare leg and jostled me for a better hold. A broad grin spread over his perfectly formed lips as he spun us in a circle.

When he stopped spinning, he simply gazed into my eyes. My senses took hold with the feel of warm skin over taut muscles. I flattened my palms over his chest and ran them up and down. He felt so solid I couldn't help it. I also couldn't help but remember our dance. Oh God. Was he about to give me another orgasm? I felt my cheeks heat with the memory of the night before. I hoped not…mostly. "Your mother is watching."

"No one can see anything." Underwater, his fingers sank into my thighs. His mouth opened and his lips brushed mine. "Violet," he murmured then dove deeper into the kiss and into the ocean, water nearing his chest and mine. We were far from shore, secluded and engulfed in each other.

His lips moved in a tempo that was both lazy and urgent, and in that moment everything made sense. His hands skimmed my back under the water, the exquisite sensation tingling every nerve. Liquid heat raced through my veins and pumped through a heart working overtime, reaching for some ending that I couldn't see over the open water or sandy shore.

I ran my fingers through his hair, lightly scraping with my nails and luxuriating in the thick locks. I didn't know where this kiss would take us, but I knew one thing for certain: We could never go back.

Minutes passed. Maybe more. His tongue slid in and seduced my mouth. I opened for him. He settled me against, the hardness and heat of him causing me to shudder. I lasciviously rocked into him.

Tiny gasps and little moans escaped us as the soft waves swayed our bodies. Tension ebbed and flowed. Time ticked. Faint sounds like kids playing and boats passing filtered in, but it all just added to the moment of him and us. Once again on this beach we were the only two people in existence. And whatever it was between us was the only thing that mattered.

Finally he pulled back, his chest heaving in a deep and powerful rhythm. His arms tightened around me and his deep gaze found me.

I whispered, "What are we doing, Jared?"

"We're just riding the waves, blossom. Just riding the waves."

I gazed deep into his eyes. "I don't want to just ride the waves with you. I want to cross the sea."

Chapter Fifteen

Jared

Whack! Whack!

I steadied a two-by-four over the makeshift workbench and centered the nail. A drop of sweat dripped on the sheet of plywood.

Whack!

Using my forearm, I wiped my forehead to keep sweat from running into my eyes. Maybe if I hammered the damn plywood hard enough, I'd work out yesterday's frustration. Yesterday? What about the night before that? Hell. Let's just call it this whole damn week's frustration. Regardless of when it was, I needed relief.

Whack!

As if that were even possible.

It wasn't. There was only one cure for what ailed me, and she was inside making lunch. My groin was a coiled spring wound so tight it was ready to explode from the middle. That wouldn't be pretty for anyone. I picked up another ten-penny nail.

Whack!

That one left a dent.

For Christ's sake, what had I been thinking yesterday kissing her at the beach? That hadn't been the nastiest part of it. Thank God, Mom had called out to us or I was certain I might've said something untrue and unforgivable, like I was falling in love with her. Christ. What's worse, I would've meant it. And what about two nights ago dancing her right into an orgasm? Watching her take her pleasure and knowing I'd given it. "Whew."

My body had stood hard and throbbing for so long it was a wonder my other extremities survived the lack of blood flow.

But Violet. Oh God. Violet. I groaned. She'd opened for me, blossomed just like I'd imagined she would. She'd come right there on the dance floor and right in my arms. Her head thrown back and her creamy neck begging to be tasted. My body stirred again. I licked my cracking lips. She'd been a dream, a goddess. I couldn't have resisted if someone had held a gun to my head.

I didn't need a firearm. What I needed was this hammer to knock some sense back into me. Right up against my temple.

Whack! Whack!

I couldn't keep kidding myself. This wasn't just about sex. Not anymore. I could get sex anywhere if I needed it. But that wasn't what I needed. This was different. My mind was flipping like a marlin on a hook. A strange tightness banded my chest again, the unwelcome sensation becoming all too familiar. I shook off my leather work gloves, letting them fall to the ground.

No. This wasn't about sex. The damn woman had snagged some locked-up part of me I'd thought I'd buried years ago. *"Idiot."*

I grabbed my bottled water and took a swig. From the moment I'd met her, I'd know she was trouble. And it hadn't been a matter of *if*. It had been only a matter of *when*. She'd gotten to my groin with her deep-blue eyes and her sexy body just like any beautiful female naturally would've. But now, I couldn't get her off my mind—and my thoughts weren't about banging her. A tremor ran down my spine. My heart still tripped when I remembered her with Mom, seeing her help and care, laugh and joke. Damn it. *"Moron."*

Here I was again, the scene from the beach playing out like one of her crap romances. She wanted to cross the sea with me. That wasn't going to happen. She could forget it. I rode waves and moved on. That's what I did. I didn't stick around for a voyage.

The real problem had started when she'd opened up and shared about her father's death and the effect it had on her. My heart had cracked open. Deep thunderous desire to keep her safe and calm her fears had crashed over me. The idea of marriage to her even popped into my head. No wonder I'd shot up out of the sand like a bullet.

Marriage? God almighty, where in creation had that thought come from? Who knew? All I knew was that she had a dream of a family and a home, and in that moment of insanity, I wanted to give it to her; I craved to give it to her. But thank the heavens, what sense I'd had remaining had come to the forefront. How could I tell her that I'd lost my heart a long time ago and there was nothing left for her to win?

"Hello there, Jared."

I spun to my left to see Mr. Callahan standing in his yard on the other side of the chain-link fence. I dropped the hammer on my workbench and walked over. "Hey, Mr. C. How's it going?"

"We're doing all right. Margerie's had a bad case of the gout, but otherwise we can't complain."

"Hope she's feeling better."

"Oh she is. She is. You in town for the big to-do?"

"Yep. I was just finishing up the talent-show platform." I kicked at a weed in the grass and gestured toward my worktable. "You and Mrs. C coming?"

He smiled and nodded. "Oh yes. Me, Margerie, and Alex. We plan on being there."

The hair on the back of my neck stood again. "Alex is coming?"

Alexis and Mr. and Mrs. Callahan had been a part of our Fourth of July celebrations from the time we'd been in grade school all the way through high school. Every year up until she married. "Is Rob coming too?"

Mr. Callahan narrowed his eyes, his lips thinning into a straight line. "You haven't heard, then?"

My heart began to pound heavy in my chest. I shook my head. "Heard what?"

"Alex filed for divorce two months ago."

I pulled the ball cap off my head and pushed my wet hair back. *Divorced?* I couldn't catch my breath. That was wrong. Alex wasn't the type to give up. Never had been.

"She and a group of women caught the bastard messing with one of the choir members in the church offices. Big scandal. The senior pastor let him go. Heard he went north trying to find a job in Vero Beach. He'll have to go farther than that, I think."

I blinked and shielded my eyes from the sun with my hand. How could that have happened? "I hadn't heard. I-I'm sorry." My head was swimming.

"Alex is looking for a job. She considered calling you, but wasn't sure…" He glanced sheepishly to his feet.

I'd bet my balls Alex would've wrung his neck if she knew he'd shared that little tidbit. "Have her call me. If I can't find her a position at SC Endeavors, I'm sure Nathaniel has something locally within the hotels."

"You know, her mother and I had always hoped… Aw, well, doesn't matter. So I understand you're nearly engaged yourself."

"Huh?" I braced myself against the fence. What in the hell was he—oh, right. "Yes." The declaration came out more emphatically than intended. "Maybe."

I hadn't had a wedding vision in my mind for a long time. A long time, if I didn't count that insanity yesterday. But now a wedding would be possible. If Alex was divorced, the idea was conceivable. I tried to conjure the long-forgotten image of being married to Alex. The vision wouldn't come.

"Heard about Cathy."

I snapped back to the conversation. "Oh. Yes."

"I think Margerie's been bringing over food on Tuesdays." Mr. C took a deep breath and let it out in a sigh. "Damn shame, if you ask me. Ought to be something they can do."

I couldn't disagree. "It's not what we'd hoped for."

"I know Alex and her prayer group have Cathy on their list every week." He draped his forearm across the aluminum bar. "Can't say enough about how sad and sorry I am, son." He held out the hand for me. "We'll see you next week."

I took it and shook it gently, clearing my throat. "Thanks, Mr. C."

He strode to the house, still as confident and strong as ever. The man had aged, but when I looked at him, I saw the closest thing to a father I'd ever known. There'd been a time I'd believed he was family, or that he would be eventually. But that had all ended when Alex married.

But she wasn't married anymore, or wouldn't be as soon as the divorce was final. That was a gut-kicker. My heart had continued to pound, and my addled mind tossed in different directions. Alex divorced. Unmarried. Free.

I pinched my bottom lip between my thumb and forefinger, getting a foul taste of sweat and leather for my trouble. Could a relationship even be possible after more than a dozen years? She had a daughter. Hell, I hadn't even seen Alex in five years. Even then it'd been a brief conversation in the front yard during my stay over Christmas a few years back. She'd been with Rob.

Christ, I hated that man. Now even more than I had. Vero Beach wasn't far. I could find him. My hand fisted at my side.

"Jared."

The sound of my name jerked me out of my ass-kicking fantasy. The back door stood open, Violet's head poked out. "Lunch is almost ready. Get washed up."

"Kinda bossy, aren't you?"

She dazzled me with a smile, her plump bottom lip stretching to reveal straight teeth. "It's the only thing that gets your attention."

"Not the only thing," I muttered. A growl formed low in my chest. I wanted to nip that sassy lip.

"Don't dawdle."

The screen door slammed shut.

My mind might be in the past, but my body, especially the lower regions, was having none of it. My perfect match, huh? We might have to double-check that.

Chapter Sixteen

Violet

Several incident-free days had passed since the kiss in the ocean and my dance floor extravaganza with Jared. For the most part, we played the loving couple in public but barely spoke in private. Since that one afternoon at the beach when everything had changed. Or at least for me it had.

In fact, a knot had begun to form in my stomach. Something had happened, and that something had caused Jared to back away. Gone were his lewd innuendos, improper propositions, and affection of any kind. He was steering as far clear as he could. And I knew exactly why.

Not that I thought his retreat was a bad thing. It wasn't. I was glad. Ok, that was a bold-faced lie. The truth was I should've been glad—it was the perfect opportunity to get my defenses back in place. But I wasn't glad. I was worried, anxious. Hurt.

"Blossom, would you help me set the table for supper?"

I spun toward Cathy and smiled. "Of course."

In the last few days, she'd come to rely on me more and more. And I loved spending time with her. With Jared's retreat, there had been a lot of time to do that.

The memory of Jared's kiss swamped my brain for the fortieth time. Whatever was between us had the tow of a riptide. That kiss had consumed us both and I'm not sure where it would've stopped if we'd been alone.

But it was the look on his face when I told him I wanted more from him. It was almost as if—

"Jared finally got the folding table set up in the living room."

I jerked out of the memory with a jump, and just like she had that afternoon on the beach, Cathy pretended nothing had happened. And after that kiss nothing *had* happened. No more yoga lessons or dirty dancing, except practicing our routine for the talent show, but even then Jared made certain that either Cathy or Mari was present—to help, he said.

"Penny'll be here any minute. I want to get the good dishes out and cover the table." Cathy smiled at me, but I could tell she wasn't feeling well this morning. Still, like a brave trooper she was putting up a good front.

"Right. Sure. Of course." I sounded rattled and out of breath. I tended to after reliving that kiss, which I had many times, but still I followed her over to a small china hutch in the corner of the living room.

Jared had scooted the sofa and coffee table back against a far wall and set the long table in its place. The thing spanned from nearly one end of the room to the other.

"Alejandro and I bought this hutch at a yard sale a week before we moved into this house. We had to keep it in the motel room until we moved it. Lord, what a pain." She smiled wistfully. "But we were so proud to have it. It was the first piece of furniture either of us had ever owned."

She bent and pulled open the bottom drawer. "You can pull all the plates out. There should be ten."

I hurried to make sure she wouldn't try and lift them herself. In the last week, I'd found the woman had a stubborn streak in her. "Let me get those."

I carefully pulled an antique set of china from the drawer and set them on the table behind me. The plates were trimmed in gold and had green vines with tiny pink blossoms around the edges. "They're beautiful."

She ran a finger across one and frowned. "And dusty. We'll need to wash them before we eat on them."

"Did you buy the hutch to hold the china?"

Pushing the bottom drawer closed with her foot, she opened the top with her hand. "No. We bought it to hold this." She pulled out a white lace tablecloth from its nesting place inside.

"Wow. That's gorgeous and old."

"It was Alejandro's. It was one of the few things he carried with him from Nicaragua, and the only thing he left behind."

I ran my hand across it. Though handmade, the workmanship was exquisite. It didn't surprise me he'd carried it with him but it did surprise me that he'd left it.

"I think he was in such a hurry to leave, he forgot it." She humphed softly as if remembering something. "I'd planned on giving it to Jared's wife." Her gaze boldly met mine.

A rush of heat flooded my cheeks. I cleared my throat and chuckled nervously. "You'd have better luck giving it to Mari."

"No." She never released my gaze. "It belongs with Jared."

The front door opened.

"Knock, knock." A tall woman, younger than Cathy but with the same eyes and nose, poked her head in.

Cathy released me from her gaze and smiled at the woman. "Hello there, old lady."

Penny hurried over to her and squeezed her in a tight hug. "Who you calling old? I'm three years younger than you." She pulled back and surveyed Cathy. "How're you feeling?"

"Pretty good. Had to wear the oxygen for the last three days."

Penny frowned. "You should've been doing that anyway."

"Come on and sit down," Cathy said, effectively changing the subject.

I knew quite a few of her tactics by now. I chuckled under my breath.

Penny glanced up and took notice of me. "Hi, I'm Penny Williams, Cathy's younger sister." She stressed the word *younger*.

I laughed and took her outstretched hand. "Violet Murphy."

Her eyes widened. "Jarry's fiancée." She narrowed her eyes and gave me a sly smile. "You must have something special for that hound dog to settle down."

If she only knew the truth. "Well, we're not exactly engaged."

She flitted her hand, as if that were of no consequence. "A matter of time, honey."

I guess we would see.

Chapter Seventeen

Violet

Cathy's extended family had descended on the house in the last two days. People came and went in an ebb and flow crowd.

It was great being around so many family members. It was also stressful—keeping up with names, dodging frolicking kids running in and out, and keeping up an acceptable appearance.

In the humidity, my hair kinked up like a bad porno flick, and my pasty skin trembled with fear in the Florida sun. After yoga, I started each morning with a full-body application of SPF 50, but that didn't seem like enough for my pale self. During an eye-opening trip to the grocery store with Mari and her kids, I'd looked for SPF 100, but apparently they don't make that. Fifty would have to do.

I was certain the sun had telescoped in and we were all destined to burn to death. The heat was something I couldn't remember experiencing. At least not to this extent. But being on the beach was worth putting up with the sun. Because we lived near Lake Michigan, Mom and I had always gone to the mountains for vacation. But the beach was different.

With Penny's arrival came her son, Devon, who a few years older than Jared; his wife, Donna; their thirteen-year-old girl, Daphne; and twin boys, Ben and Cole, who looked to be about six.

Cathy's older sister, Julie, had also come with her family. At least three of her children—she had five—and seven grandchildren of varying ages. I fell in love with Uncle Ed, her husband, who liked to tell bad jokes at the table and sprayed the kids with a water gun he'd brought from home.

The house was a noisy wreck with people in and out, and the backyard was even worse. Jared and Devon had set up a gathering place under the canopy where snacks and drinks littered long folding tables.

Gone were the china and lace tablecloths, which had given way to paper plates and plastic tableware, and, of course, the obligatory red Solo cup.

A stark-naked, dripping four-year-old streaked by me. I held my beer aloft to keep from spilling it on the little bugger. He tore down the hill, across the street toward the beach.

"Jeremy, come back here. You forgot your swimsuit." His mother marched far behind.

That caused a roar of laughter from the older people in the peanut gallery.

Uncle Ed yelled, "You did the same thing in this very yard, Glenda."

She turned to glare at him. "I most certainly did not." His daughter's face turned a bright shade of pink and everyone laughed again.

It had been like this for two days, and tonight everyone had gathered for the fireworks, which, I'd been told, could be seen in awe-inspiring wonder from the backyard.

The sun had just barely started its decent from high in the sky, and smoke from the grill wafted through the backyard. Jared stood over the open flame tossing hamburger patties and hot dogs on. The red-and-white checkered apron he wore made me smile.

"Each year he gets more and more handsome. He looks just like his father."

I turned to look over my shoulder at his Aunt Julie. "You met him?"

"Several times." She nodded. "I was the only one who ever did. I was out of the house by then, working in Miami. I drove up in my new car, a green Suzuki Samurai." She shook her head, smiling. "I'd never seen a couple more in love than Cath and Al. Mari had just been born and they had fixed up the house. I was so jealous. Ed and I were dating, but I knew we didn't have what they had."

"Apparently you had something better."

Catching my meaning, she smiled. "Yes. It will be thirty-one years in September. But I couldn't imagine it at the time. None of us could."

"What do you think happened?"

"I think that Alejandro was a man with a single-minded heart. He was as passionate as he was careless. He couldn't hold his love for his country and his love for his family in it at the same time."

"But he married again. How do you explain that?"

"Well, for one, he didn't have to choose, did he?"

That was true.

"And I don't believe he loved the woman he married, not like he loved Cathy. I just don't see someone loving like that more than once in a lifetime."

"But if he loved her so much, why would he leave?"

"That is a mystery I've never been able to solve. I tried convincing myself that he'd never really cared for them, but I couldn't ever make myself believe it. Neither could Cath. We'd seen him… We may never know." Her face suddenly clouded and her voice came out as a whisper. "What is *she* doing here?"

I turned my head to see who Julie was looking at. An older couple I recognized as the neighbors were talking with Jared, but his gaze was focused on the thin blonde standing next to them. *Alex.*

Chapter Eighteen

Jared

"Hey, Daph, can you bring me that big platter on the kitchen counter?"

Smoke rose from the flame as I flipped the burgers, the sizzle giving me male satisfaction. Burning flesh over an open fire. A rite of passage for any American man.

Uncle Ed usually cooked the Fourth of July evening meal, but he'd handed over his apron and man-sized spatula then taken a seat in the shade with a cold beer. I was beginning to think I'd been the fool. The heat from the grill made sweat stream down my back and the smoke caused my eyes to water and burn.

"Hello, Jared."

The voice slid over me like satin. A chill raced up and down my arms. I closed the lid on the burgers to find an older, world-wizened, more beautiful Alex in my sights. I shook off a shiver.

"Hey, girl. Where have you been?" I stepped around the grill and hugged her.

She felt soft and dainty, cool in my arms. I pulled back and suppressed a satisfied smile. Her cheeks held a definite blush. My heart pounded ninety miles an hour. I winked at her and tried to step back behind the grill, putting some distance between us.

Before I could get away, Mrs. C pulled me in for a hug too. "Hey, handsome. Why haven't you come by to see me? I had my famous brownies waiting on you."

Mr. C frowned. "She slapped my hand more than once when I'd tried to take one."

Couldn't help but chuckle. "Nobody told me. I'd have been over in a minute if I'd known there were brownies."

"I brought some with me." She held out a container. "Mel said he caught you working in the yard last week."

"He did."

She grasped my arm. "We're so sorry, Jared. We love your mother and you." Her eyes glistened and her voice broke.

"I know, Mrs. C." A lump formed in my throat.

"Helen, stop that. This is a day for celebrating."

"I know *I'm* celebrating." Alex reached into the cooler and pulled out a beer. "It's a real Independence Day for me." She held up the bottle in a toast. "My divorce was final on Friday."

Another shiver ran through me. "I heard about that. I'm sorry, Al."

"I'm not. Not anymore." She took a long swig. "So what have you been up to? I heard you were getting married."

"What?" I scanned the mingling crowd. Violet caught my gaze and smiled, but the interest and intensity in her eyes was more than casual. And her right brow twitched. She was jealous. That earned her a broad smile, and reading it for what it was, she rolled her eyes.

"Is that her?"

I turned my attention back to Alex. "That's Violet, but we're not engaged."

Alex's gaze met mine in an electric charge, creating more tightening tension in my chest. Mixing women—that's what I did. What I was used to. Some would even call it my specialty. But if there was one thing I knew instinctively, it was that these two women would never mix.

"Here's your platter, dear cousin." Daphne set it down on the table next to the grill.

"Daph, you remember the Callahans, right?"

She smiled at Mr. and Mrs. C. "Of course. How've you been?"

The older couple went into a spiel about high blood pressure, gout, and a bout with the shingles.

Alex stepped around them. "I've heard this story."

"I bet." I smiled and shoveled the burgers and dogs onto the plate and set it on the table. "Come and get it," I hollered to the crowd.

The horde descended like locusts, leaving Alex and I to move away or be trampled.

The years had been good to her. Her skin was still tan and smooth, but her face was strained and she carried a few laugh lines around her eyes, which were still the color of dark amber whiskey. "Guess they were hungry."

"Guess so" was all I could say.

We stood under the gate, hidden and forgotten by the others, our gazes locked, and a dozen years of conversation hung unsaid between us. My heart pounded.

Alex cleared her throat and turned toward the ocean. "I should go check on Bethany. I told her she could go to the water and that I'd be down in a minute."

Restless apprehension raced inside me. I warred with indecision. For the first time in years, in maybe my life, I didn't know what I wanted. Damn it. I leaned back to search the backyard.

My gaze fell immediately on what I sought. Violet had a paper plate in her hand and was apparently fixing one of the twins a hot dog, because she leaned over him, pointing to the mustard or ketchup. The boy grinned up and said something that made her laugh.

The fire that had begun in my heart, which I'd tried to smother, suffocate, and even the other day in the water see if I could burn out, blazed to life again. I couldn't deny I felt something real for this woman. I wanted her. But not in a way I'd ever imagined wanting a woman. Not even in the way I'd wanted Alex. I wanted Violet beside me, watching movies, laughing with the family, taking a walk, or going on vacation. I wanted her laundry mixed with mine. Her shampoo in my shower. I wasn't going to lie, I wanted her in my bed…but mostly I wanted her in my life.

I turned back to Alex and smiled. "I'll go with you." I couldn't deny what I felt for her either. I'd spent years dreaming of her, imagining us together. Just because I'd developed feelings for another woman I'd known less than a year didn't mean I could swipe the rest from my mind like a dry-erase board. If I was ever going to have anything real with either of them, I needed to pack away the past. That was what this trip was about, right? Saying good-bye.

"You don't have to. I know you have guests."

"I want to." I took her hand. "I need to, Al."

She laced her fingers together with mine, and just like we'd done a thousand times when we were kids, we walked the trail to the beach.

The years melted away as the sun set behind us.

Alex and I never minced words. I saw no reason to now. I needed answers, and she could finally give them. "Why did you marry him, Al?"

It wasn't the first time I'd asked the question, but the last time I'd asked it was the week before her wedding, the last time we'd truly talked as best friends. She hadn't answered me then. Not really.

She kicked at the sand on the edge of grass, and pulled me toward two spread towels and a folding chair. "That's Beth's stuff."

The beach crowd had thinned, but late swimmers still played in the waves. We sat on the towels. Alex waved to a cute little blonde about eight or nine at the edge of the water.

"I let her play alone as long as the water doesn't go over her knees. Usually she just likes to build sandcastles." She sighed. "Don't we all."

"She looks just like you."

Alex chuckled. "That's what everyone says, but I can't see it myself. She is the best thing I've ever done."

I nodded.

Several waves crashed on shore, the tide pulling out for the evening. My question wasn't forgotten, and I could feel the tension coiling in her as she struggled to form a response.

Finally, she turned her head to me. "Because I knew Rob was in love with me. I knew I could have the kind of safe life I'd always wanted."

"You didn't think I could give you that?"

"I knew you couldn't, Jared." Her words came out in a frustrated gasp. "You had changed during senior year."

"How? How had I changed? I was still your best friend."

"Yes. And no. Jared, your body had begun to fill out. It was clear to not only me, but every girl in school that you were coming into your own. My God, I can't even tell you how many girls asked me about you at graduation. 'Are you dating Jared?' 'Is he seeing anyone?' 'Could you give him my number?' And not just the high school girls. It was their college-aged sisters, and sometimes even their aunts."

She shook her head. "It didn't take me long to figure out the scene. You were going away to college. I was staying here. Even if we'd decided to…" She dug trenches in the sand by her leg. "I knew it would've never lasted. And I wasn't prepared to live with that, Jared."

"So you accepted Burns instead. Did you love him?"

"I thought I did. He swept me off my feet. He was sweet, attentive, romantic. He promised me a lot. And if I couldn't talk to him the way I'd talked to you, well…that was just the price I had to pay for getting the life I wanted."

"Did you love me?" I didn't want to know the answer to the question. I knew it would once again break my heart.

"Mama. Mama. Watch this." Bethany was yelling from the shore.

Alex swiped away a tear, smiled at the girl, and lifted her hand. "I see you, baby."

The tiny blonde dove into a wave, her legs coming straight out of the water in a perfect handstand before another wave knocked her over in a back flip.

"Yes." Alexis's voice was barely a whisper. "Every single day."

I blew out a shaky breath. "But not enough to give me a chance, to trust me with your heart. I would've done anything for you." I couldn't suppress the rage I felt. I wanted to fight, and yell.

Tears shone in her eyes. "I'm sorry, Jared. I thought I was making the best choice. The right choice at the time. I thought I was making the safe choice."

"How could you have thought that?" I dug my fingers into the sand to keep from pounding it. "You knew me. Better than anyone. How could you imagine I wouldn't treasure you and keep your heart safe?"

"I know, right?" A humorless laugh escaped with a few tears. "What a joke. And now it's too late."

She met my gaze, hope clinging there, as if I could make it all better. All I felt was anger. Anger at myself for wasting so many years wishing for a girl who'd never trusted me. For Alex I felt only sadness. In her eyes lingered the hope of second chance, but I couldn't help her with that. I could only help her move on.

"Your dad said you were looking for a job."

The emotion she'd revealed vanished, shuttered behind a placid amber gaze. She wrapped her arms around herself. "Yes. I am. Do you know of any?"

"I might if you're willing to relocate to Chicago."

"Actually, I'd love a fresh start somewhere. This town is too small. I need somewhere nobody knows my name."

My heart pounded heavy against my ribs. I might not still want her, but that didn't mean I wasn't curious about certain things. "You'll have to undergo some significant personality testing, but if you have Internet access, I can get you those tonight and we can see if you fit any of our openings."

She smiled again, and this time it was filled with gratitude. "Thank you. I'd head home right now if it meant a guarantee of starting over."

I chuckled. "I can guarantee you a position. We just need to find the right fit. I think I can vouch for your character."

She pushed my shoulder, gently knocking me sideways. "I would hope so since I am your oldest and dearest friend. And probably the only girl on the face of the planet you've known more than ten minutes and haven't kissed or made a pass at."

That really did make me laugh. "True, but I'm thinking it might be time to settle down."

"The new girl?" She blew out a shaky breath. "Mom said her name is Violet."

"Yep. Violet."

"So you're not going to tell me about her?"

"Nope."

She laughed. "Okay. I understand."

I wasn't sure she did. If I didn't understand myself, how could she? All I knew was that I wanted to be with Violet. Something had begun to change between the two of us from the moment this trip started, and I didn't want it to end here. I wouldn't let it end here. "I better get back to the house."

Alex nodded in understanding. "I'll get Beth, and we'll be up in a minute to eat before the show." She took a deep breath and looked up at the sky. "The sun is setting. The fireworks will start soon. Talent show is tomorrow, right?"

"That it is."

She shot me an assessing look. "I don't suppose you have a talent to reveal?"

"As a matter of fact, I do, and it promises to be epic."

"Even more epic than the time we did a skit from *Pee-Wee's Big Adventure*?"

I groaned and fell back on the sand. "I spent eighty dollars of my yard money to rent that costume."

"And…w-when…when…" She was laughing so hard she could barely catch her breath, let alone speak. "When your trousers…fell down…r-right as you lifted your leg to get on the tricycle."

A burst of laugher erupted from my lips. "Yes. That was pretty epic. And wasn't it good of Uncle Ed to catch it all on video?"

She wiped both the sad and happy tears from her eyes. "Lord, I haven't laughed like that in…I can't remember when." She turned her head to see me. "Thanks, Jared. And I know tomorrow will be another era of epic talent."

"Are you and Bethany coming back for the show?"

She ducked her head and bit her lip. "If we're welcome."

Using my nickname for her for the first time in over a decade, I said, "Ally Bally, you can only come on one condition: You have to participate." I winked at her.

She laughed again. "You're a turkey butt, you know that?"

"A turkey butt? No. Can't say I've ever been called that before." My laughter stopped. "I'm sorry about what happened to you, Al. You didn't deserve what Rob did to you. And as long as we meet here, you and Bethany will always be welcome."

She grabbed my shoulders and hugged me. "Thank you."

I pulled away, dusted the sand from my legs, and headed back.

Chapter Nineteen

Violet

I finished up my morning yoga routine and headed for some coffee. Jared had shown me a couple of other moves, and the past few mornings I'd found the exercise helpful in getting through the chaos of the days. But not this morning.

Jared's cousins were coming out of the woodwork like cockroaches, and I meant that in the nicest way possible. But it was true. They were everywhere. A group of the kids had decided on a game of hide-and-seek this morning. Two of the little darlings had insisted on using the top bunk as their hidey spot. While I was still in it!

Jared, still sleeping in the bottom bunk, had shooed them away, but I was seriously contemplating a can of bug spray.

Hence my deep-breathing exercises. Unhelpful.

Last night had been the worst night with Jared since I'd been here. And the best. Confusion swirled inside me and my mind was still reeling.

That woman from next door had come to the party and stolen Jared away while her mother had proceeded to tell us of the scandal and Alexis's subsequent divorce. Which made me, for all intents and purposes, obsolete.

I stood up from the floor and wiped the sweat off my neck. I was a big girl. I could admit that it bothered me a little…a lot. Actually, I'd wanted to scratch Alex's ugly brown eyes out and dump her flailing body far in the ocean where she may or may not wash back up on shore.

Finally, after the sun had set and the stars came out, Jared had returned to the backyard without Ms. Girl-Next-Door.

I'd been relieved not to have to commit murder, but I hadn't been wholly at ease either. Until he'd grabbed a blanket and me, spreading us both out on the grass in the corner of the yard.

He'd lain next to me and pulled my head to his chest. "Have to put on a good show for the family, you know."

"Of course. Wouldn't want to disappoint." But nothing in my life had ever felt more real than that moment. The heat of his skin, the smell of him, the sound of his heart beating in my ear and the pop and spray of multicolored fireworks overhead.

All of these were dreams I'd never let myself imagine about anyone. Especially not Casanova Cassidy.

I'd subtly asked about how things had gone at the beach, and in usual Jared fashion, he'd brushed it off as insignificant.

At the end of the display, he'd bent his head and brushed the corner of my mouth with a tender kiss, and I was lost. I'd wanted to pull him in for more. But the craziest part of the entire night was that I'd known he'd been swept away too. I felt it. Something had changed, had loosened, and I sensed an openness in him I'd never sensed before. My heart soared to heights I knew my reality could never support.

I didn't know why I even bothered with the yoga this morning. My heart was ramming out a steady clip already. I'd run the scene over in my head a hundred times since waking. I fanned my T-shirt to cool my body. The exercise was nothing but a rehash of all my emotions, and thoughts of Jared. How could anyone find their inner peace with thoughts of Jared breathing down their neck? Actually, the thoughts *were* of Jared breathing down my neck. He hadn't strayed from my mind more than two minutes since…well, I couldn't remember since when. Since we'd embarked on this trip, probably. But this morning, it had been impossible to clear him from my head. And if I was honest, my heart.

I slipped down the hall, trying to avoid the miniature mob of kids, and headed for a cup of much-needed coffee. At the moment, the house appeared quiet, but I knew it could be an ambush. Maybe they'd all gone to the water. I tiptoed to the kitchen, peeking inside.

A shirtless Jared, wearing board shorts and flip-flops, had his back turned. His cell phone was pressed to his ear and he was stirring sugar into a cup of coffee.

A flush of warm excitement covered me head to chest. Wanting nothing more than to watch—or to lick, either one would work—I leaned against the doorframe, admiring the muscles in his back and shoulders that flexed when he shifted.

"As soon as you get the results, I want to see them. Send them to my email. I'll print them here. But remember, I don't want her results to become part of the database. For my eyes only, understand?"

He must be talking to someone at work. Dr. Huxtley most likely. It was strange. Normally, email and voicemail would be blowing up if we were out for even just a few hours, but I hadn't received any messages from the office the whole time we'd been gone—going on a week and a half now. Jared had only gotten a few calls from Scorge and Maddie keeping him updated. I figured they wanted him to have this time with his family, with his mother, uninterrupted, and had forbidden anyone from contacting us.

"Yeah. I want to see those too. And tell Nathaniel we *will* find a place for Alexis, even if we have to create a new position." He laughed. "I know that's not your place, Hux."

Alexis? My heart sank into my tossing stomach, and my breath snagged in my throat. The fine hairs on my arms and at the back of my neck rose in protest. He was giving Alex a job? In Chicago? No. It couldn't be.

I stormed back to the room and contemplated packing. "Violet, you're an idiot. This is what he does."

I paced in front of the bunks. "You knew what he was like." I lifted my arms in frustration and let them slap back to my sides. "Why? Why, then, did you let down your guard? Why did you let him in?" If I'd eaten anything I would've puked it up.

I plopped down on the side of the bottom bed and dropped my head in my hands.

"Hey. There you are."

"Here I am."

"I brought you some coffee." Jared handed me the mug and sat, his arm going around my shoulders. "What's up?"

I stood up, breaking the contact. "So you're finding Alexis a job in Chicago." I didn't phrase it as a question because I knew the answer. "That'll be convenient. Her mom told us last night she's divorced."

"It's not what you think, Vi."

"Not what I think? Not what I think? Seriously, Jared?" I narrowed my eyes at him. "Did you really just say that? For reals, really?"

"Vi, stop it."

"You clearly don't owe me an explanation. I'm a paid companion. Purchased for the sole purpose of fooling your mother—"

"Would you just listen?"

And just to be mean, I added, "—who isn't fooled, by the way. She's known all along what you were up to."

That stopped him. "What do you mean she's known all along?"

"The first day she confessed to me that she knew what we were about. She knows you were trying to trick her."

"Damn it." He rubbed a cheek covered in sexy overnight stubble, which I was, from this moment on, refusing to notice. "I should've known. I never could fool her. But then why didn't she say anything?"

I rolled my eyes. "Because she's hoping that by the end of the visit, our relationship won't be pretend."

He sat there staring at the floor for a moment. He looked up and met my eyes with his liquid-brown gaze.

Tingles zipped over my skin. I steeled myself against them and his stare. "Well, one girl is just as good as another. I'm sure she'll be just as pleased to hear about—"

He yanked me to him on the bed and covered my mouth, kissing me thoroughly before pulling away. "Now can I talk?" His tone was harsh, but his arms kept me anchored to his lap.

Not having regained my powers of speech, I nodded.

"Good." His voice gentled. "I'm not getting back with Alexis. I'm helping her find a job. That's all." He narrowed his eyes, scrutinizing me. "Do you believe me or do I need to kiss you again?"

While I wouldn't mind another one of those kisses, I shook my head, still unable to talk.

"Okay." He released me and then stood and began pacing in front of the bunks using the exact same path I'd just been pacing. A smile tugged at his lips. "She's something else, isn't she?" He looked up. "My mother?"

I smiled back, remembering our long conversations. "She's pretty amazing. I'm glad I've gotten to know her."

I had been concerned about Cathy for the last couple of days. She had stayed in her room most of the time and had only come out briefly for the evening festivities. The circles under her eyes indicated more than just exhaustion and I wondered how wise it had been to have such a large crowd. But still, she seemed glad everyone was here and had not uttered a word of complaint.

"Me too."

"That alone was worth the trip down here."

He stepped close again. "That's the only thing about this trip you've enjoyed? Meeting my mom?" His husky voice breezed over my cheek and he nuzzled his nose in my hair.

My heart began to thunder, this time prepared for...something.

Reaching up, Jared tenderly stroked my jaw, letting out a small private sigh. He held my gaze for a moment as if he were about to reveal some secret and then thought better of it. Then he said, "We need to practice before the talent show.

Chapter Twenty

Jared

I craned my head around the corner of the house into the backyard.

"Lemme see, Uncle Jared. Lemme see." Corey tugged on the hem of my black T-shirt.

"You've already had your turn. Go sit with your mother."

Violet slapped me on the arm. I swung my head around to scowl at her.

"He's not bothering anybody."

I frowned down at the four-year-old, then back up at Vi. "Speak for yourself."

"Honey, Uncle Jared is in a foul mood. He's nervous—"

"I am not nervous."

She rolled her eyes and ignored me. She did that quite a bit so I was used to it. "He is and I want you to see our dance so go sit with Mommy, okay?"

He smiled up at her. "'kay, Aunt Viwet."

I startled. "Since when are you Aunt Viwet?"

"Since your niece and nephew decided they like me better than you," she pronounced with smug satisfaction.

"As if that were possible." I craned my neck around the corner, watching the little tike settle into Mari's lap.

Daphne, mistress of ceremonies, stepped up onto the small platform. A loud squeal of feedback echoed through the speaker, which was basically a karaoke machine. "Now for the performance you've all—"

A crash of thunder rattled the house.

Crap. The clouds had been slowly creeping in. Now it seemed the storm was imminent.

I took Violet's hand and held my breath. Her fingers trembled. I pulled them to my lips and kissed them, getting a taste of sweet vanilla from the homemade ice cream she'd eaten earlier. Ours was the last performance of the night—and the one all the cousins had stuck it out to see. Even under threat of rain.

"Everyone give a warm round of applause for Aunt Violet and Uncle Jared."

"Again with the Aunt Violet. And since when do you get top billing?"

She shrugged. "What can I say? You're family loves me."

So do I, sweet blossom. So do I. But I would wait until later tonight to say those words out loud. I scanned her lush body in that sexy dress and licked my lips. But that didn't mean I couldn't have a little fun. "'Kate, I know my timing stinks, but I just keep thinking this thing with us is gonna go away. Maybe if I keep skating and checkin', I'll get clear.'"

"Shut up, Doug Dorsey, man with the worst timing ever." She narrowed her eyes at me.

"So if I declare my undying love, will you agree to do the Pamchenko?"

"Not a chance."

I chuckled, grabbed Vi's hand, and pulled her out on the platform just as the music started.

The crowd clapped enthusiastically and another clap of thunder sounded, this time accompanied by lightning.

"You ready?"

She smiled nervously and nodded.

We'd practiced for about an hour this morning. After I'd convinced her that nothing was happening between Alex and me. And nothing would happen. Hux had sent Alex's DataMatch results this afternoon and I'd had to laugh. I'd laughed until I'd almost broken a rib, until I'd rolled on the floor.

I placed Violet's hand firmly in mine and twirled her out just as the song's beat picked up.

You're the one thing…I can't get enough of…

Drops of rain tapped the deck. They sprinkled Violet's dress, staining with each splash. Her deep-blue gaze met mine in question. I gave her a subtle nod of assurance, and she returned it with a full-on grin. Violet Murphy was all in. Heart and soul. Which was good because the rain began coming down in sheets. The crowd began to scatter in a waterlogged frenzy, but like true professionals we danced on.

We stepped in rhythm, spun, and twisted to the music that was barely audible over the downpour. When we made it to the last step, I grabbed Violet in my arms and spun her around in celebration. "You were perfect."

"Perfectly wet."

I dropped her back to the ground and placed a soft kiss at the edge of her lips. I knew if I gave her more, I wouldn't stop. "Like I said, perfect."

We hustled under the canopy as it flapped dangerously in the gusts. Uncle Ed was taking shelter there, rolling up various extension cords. Daphne snatched up her karaoke machine and sprinted for the door.

Thunder rattled and lightning cracked. Charlie and Devon were pulling down the canopy before it blew away. Violet and I joined in the conservation efforts, trying to save tablecloths, lawn chairs, and leftover food.

Everyone had scattered either in cars heading back to their hotels or into the house.

I bent down to grab the last beer from the cooler when an icy onslaught poured over my back. I hollered and shot up, spinning to see which cousin was about to face my wrath.

Violet stood there laughing, the empty ice bucket guiltily clutched in her hand.

She dropped it, squealed like a girl, and took off for the house.

I shook off the ice still clinging to my neck and streaked after her.

Chapter Twenty-One

Violet

I was running so fast, my wet feet slipped on the tile. Holding the heeled sandals in my hand, I slid into a wall as I rounded the corner for our room, trying to keep from knocking a group of people down. I didn't stop to see who, but I was running out of gas—and real estate. Laughter tore from my panting lips and sweat mingled with water running in rivulets down my face.

I couldn't help it. Jared had been bent unsuspectingly over the cooler, and the leftover ice bucket sat there beckoning me. It was a pull I couldn't resist.

The heat and breath of Jared's body radiated into my back though he was still a step or two behind. The tension of the entire day had been building to this moment, and now it flew by in fast-forward. That is until I crossed the threshold of our room and Jared's hand glanced my waist, finding purchase in my dress. His fingers closed around a swath of fabric as my feet hit the carpet, and I stopped. Still moving at Daytona speed, Jared's body crashed into mine. The door slammed shut behind us. He encircled my waist, and we went spinning like a Latin dance he hadn't had time to teach me. My body softened and molded to his. He shielded us as we bounced off a wall and against the bunks, where we finally staggered to a halt.

Yes. This day had been culminating to this moment, but it ballooned out in my heart bigger than that, bigger than a day, a week, or even a year could hold. And I couldn't help but feel my whole life had been leading me here, to this house, this family, and this man. I gasped for breath.

His lashes dripped and sparkled in the dark. Little trails of rain trickled down his jaw. Drops fell from his black pants and dripped on my bare feet. But his hands seared my hips through the dress that now clung to me like skin.

Another roll of thunder rattled the windows. Rain beat on the roof, insulating us from everyone and everything. The sounds of the cousins scrambling to get out of the downpour filled the house. Pots and pans rattled in the kitchen. People shuffled and milled about in the hall. The refrigerator door opened and closed. But even though I could hear the sounds and see the patter of shadow feet under the door, they were backdrop. My senses were locked into the moment with Jared, whose eyes darkened with a desire that promised retribution.

My flattened palms heated against his pounding chest. Freezing shivers and scorching fire warred in me for purchase. Every conflicting emotion and argument for and against this man stood on the precipice, and I wanted to give in. God, I wanted this. I wanted him with a tempest as strong as the storm raging outside.

His gaze bore into mine. Our chests heaved, and his hand slid from my waist to cup my face. "*A Walk in the Clouds*," he whispered as his lips collapsed on mine.

His kiss was frantic, deep, lush, and it was what I'd wanted for so long, what I needed. I gave myself over to it and leaned in. Sweat and rain flavored us. I slid my hands up and around his neck, pressing my body against his. The chill on my skin dissolved, and fire burned in my lips, my breasts, and between my legs. His mouth slowly opened over mine, and his tongue penetrated in a slide of molten desire so thick I groaned. He swallowed the sound like a gulp from a fresh spring. He cupped the back of my head, and pressed his hand to my backside, fitting me to him at the three intersections of our bodies.

His lips were firm and his tongue plunged with impunity. The breath caught somewhere in my chest couldn't escape, and I finally realized my nose was obstructed. I pulled back and gasped for air.

He tilted my chin up and looked into my eyes. "I always hated the ending of that scene. Keanu Reeves was an idiot for not taking that woman to bed."

I smiled, still trying to regulate my heart rate and breathing. "That's because he was already married," I panted.

Smoothing his thumb over my cheek, he leaned in closer until our noses touched. "Well, I'm not, and I intend to take you to bed, Vi. Right now."

A startled gasp spilled from me.

His mouth closed over mine again, and his hand slid behind my back, unhooking the clasp and sliding the zipper open. I sighed and tossed my head back.

My mind spun in a thousand different directions, but my thoughts weren't nearly strong enough to overcome my desire. I wanted this man. I had from the moment I'd met him, but now that I knew him, understood him, I wanted him more than I could've ever imagined wanting someone.

I fumbled between us to the hem on his black T-shirt, finally able to grasp it and reach my hands underneath. I groaned when my fingers touched the muscled chest. Coarse hair rasped against my fingertips. I raked the flesh with my nails, and then he was the one who groaned.

"God, I want you, Violet," Jared whispered. "In my bed and in my life."

What was he saying? My foggy brain was picking up the tension coiling in him. Surely he hadn't said what I'd heard or how I'd heard it. Couldn't be. But his body was confirming his words. His lips slid over my cheek down to my bare neck as the straps fell to my waist, and a warm palm cupped and kneaded my breast.

The door crashed open, and we both jumped.

Mari let out a helpless scream. "Jared, come quick. It's Mom."

Then she was gone, and we stood there next to the bunks, half undressed in a puddle of water.

His eyes lingered on me for a heartbeat; then he turned and followed Mari.

By the time I changed clothes and cleaned up the wet mess—because we hadn't been the only two to get the floor wet—and made my way to Cathy's room, everyone but Cathy's sisters, Mari, and Jared had gone. Mabel sat in a rocker in the corner of the room. Penny and Julie sat on one side of the bed, and Mari sat on the other with Charlie.

The oxygen tubes were around Cathy's head and fitted to each nostril. An IV dripped solution slowly into her, and a monitor screen beeped and blinked as it kept track of her vitals. A jab of pain cut through me. I dug my fingernails into my thigh to hold back a sob.

Her eyes were closed. The life and vibrancy had drained from her, and the pallor of her skin shone gray in the dimly lit room. I'd never hated a sight so much in my life. It seemed as if she'd aged twenty years in one night. My chest ached, and tears stung my eyes. I rubbed my face and winced, realizing the sting may have been caused by sunburn.

Jared sat with one hip perched on the far corner of the bed, one foot propped on the sideboard and the other on the floor. His body slumped toward her. He'd also changed and was wearing basketball shorts and a T-shirt that seemed too small.

Mabel looked up from her knitting to acknowledge me with a nod. "She's resting now. I don't expect her to wake before morning."

I nodded in return. "Thanks."

Jared turned his head half a notch to see me from his peripheral vision but never met my gaze. He didn't say anything.

"Would anyone like some coffee?" I asked before helplessness and heartbreak could tear down my resistance and turn me into another puddle to be cleaned up.

Mari looked up. "I'll take a cup."

The sisters also nodded.

Thank God. I needed something to do.

****

After I'd made the coffee, I went back down the hall and entered Cathy's room. Jared had gone.

"Coffee's ready. Would anyone like me to bring a cup in here?"

"I'll take one with sugar," Julie said.

"Me too." Penny's voice broke, and she dabbed her eyes with a tissue.

Mari stood. "Charlie and I'll come out and drink a cup with you."

I took the sisters their drinks, then poured three cups and brought them to the living room on a small tray I'd seen Josie use. Unsure of what Mari took in her coffee, I included sugar packets, a small glass of milk, and artificial sweetener. The busywork of making the coffee and finding the condiments calmed my mind, which needed some occupation to steady it.

Jared had probably gone to walk the beach. The worst of the storm had passed, but the intermittent pitter-patter of rain still fell. After I drank my coffee, maybe I'd try to find him. Maybe I could offer some comfort. Everything in me wanted to.

My hands hadn't stopped shaking since the news of Cathy's collapse had come, and the tray tinkled when I set it in front of the sofa where Mari and Charlie sat. I lowered into one of the straight-backed chairs that cluttered the small room.

I picked up a steaming mug and cupped it in my hands. The warmth of it steadied me a little. The clock on the mantle chimed once. One o'clock. It had been nearly eleven when we'd come in from the talent show. Hours had flown by in a haze.

Charlie draped his arm protectively over Mari's shoulders. She leaned against him.

I could imagine what Mari was feeling, but I knew she would be all right. It was Jared I was worried about. He had no one to protect and comfort him. Except me. But I wasn't sure he'd let me. "Can you tell me what happened?"

Mari leaned forward and pulled the tray closer. She opened a little pink pack and dumped the contents in her cup. "I'm not exactly sure." Her voice was solid and steady.

Admiration for her filled me. With that one sentence and her small actions, she had given me a glimpse of her inner strength.

"One minute I was dancing with Cousin Jack, and the next, Mom was on the ground with a crowd around her. Several of the guys lifted her and carried her to the bed while Mabel prepared the IV." She looked up at me then. "That's when I came to get you and Jared."

She said "you and Jared." My heart throbbed with love for her. For all of them. She'd purposely included me, because she considered me included. A part of this tragedy, and this family. A sob burst from my lips, and tears began to stream from my eyes.

Mari stood and walked over to me. She knelt and wrapped her arms around me. "Hey there, little sister. We're going to make it through this."

I hugged Mari back and continued to cry. "It's too soon. It's all too soon. I don't want to lose her yet."

"Me either." Mari had tears sliding down her cheeks now too.

I'd done such a great job of comforting her. I laughed at the thought, but it came out a snort with all the snot in my nose from crying. Charlie handed me a box of tissue. I pulled out three. "Has anyone spoken with the doctor?"

Mari stood and took a tissue too. "Mabel did. He doesn't believe she'll make it longer than a few days. Her kidneys are shutting down, and her oxygenation is near to nothing."

"But they said three to six months. We were supposed to have at least three months," I cried, knowing it was a stupid argument.

"I know. I thought the same thing. But Mom never did anything as planned. She always refused to follow the norm. That's how her life has been from the beginning. Grandma always loved to tell the story of how Mom was born three weeks early in a cab on the way to the hospital. She could never wait."

I suppressed a sob, determined not to lose my composure again. But all I could feel was that Cathy needed to wait. I needed to know her better. I needed to hear these stories. I needed to love her.

We talked a bit more and had a second cup of coffee. Mari told me about growing up with Cathy, how hard it had been, and how amazing. Feeling a need to call my own mother, I lost my battle with the tears again. Mari and I cried together. It was the most baffling experience of my life. My grief and brokenness were a painful weight inside my chest, but the closeness and bond I felt with Mari was what I'd always hoped to have in a sister.

I let the drops roll down my cheeks, not even bothering with tissues except to blow my nose. "Do you think I should go look for Jared?"

Mari shook her head. "I think he just needs some time. He'll come back when he's ready."

Chapter Twenty-Two

Jared

It had been three days. Mom still hadn't awakened. The doctors weren't sure she ever would, but what they were sure of was that the timeframe would be short. Days at best. Maybe a week.

It felt as if someone had hollowed out my gut and had tried to replace it with empty milk cartons. I'd eaten, I thought, and probably rested. I remembered conversations from five minutes ago like they were dreams. And I was pissed. Mother-fucking mad at God, the world, the doctors, and the damn cancer. I imagined using my father as target practice for my knife-throwing skills.

Julie and Penny had stayed with Mom the first two nights, Mari last night. My stubborn sister had wanted to stay up with her again tonight, but she was an accident waiting to happen. With the aunts taking turns resting in Mari's old room, I'd sent her in to the bunk bed to sleep with Violet and promised to get her if Mom woke—or worse.

Violet had taken over all the cooking and cleaning, allowing the nurses to focus on Mom.

Marvis had come back on duty. She sat quietly in the corner.

"I'm going to be here for a while if you want to take a break."

The gray-haired woman looked up from her book. "I wouldn't mind it, but call me if there is any change."

I nodded.

She gathered up an empty coffee cup, her cross-stitch, and a book of Sudoku and left.

Every muscle in my body ached from sitting too long in this blasted chair. I stood and stretched my arms over my head, bending backwards.

"Jared."

The sound was so soft I wasn't sure I'd heard it. I spun around. Mom's eyes were open.

"Water."

I moved quickly to the bedside, checking her vitals. I poured a small cup of water and slipped the straw between her cracked lips.

She was awake. After three days, she'd finally opened her eyes.

She took several small sips, the only fluid she'd taken by mouth in days. "Sorry I ruined the talent show." Her voice came out in a rasp.

I took her frail but warm hand in mine. "It's just like you to cause trouble," I teased softly.

That earned me a weak smile. She closed her eyes, and I held my breath, watching for her chest to rise and fall. I shot a look at the monitor, which continued to beep in rhythm.

Finally her eyes opened again. "I was waiting for you. It's time for me to go."

"I don't want you to go, Mom." I held back an onslaught of tears with a fury.

"But it's not up to you, son."

"No. It's not." Shades of that awful day when I was four came rushing back. I hated my father for leaving, but I never wanted to hate my mother. I wanted to throw the glass vase of flowers against the wall just to hear it shatter, but I held back and I listened, letting my heart break as it would.

"When I first got sick, I prayed that God would let me see you settled. I wasn't afraid of dying, but I was afraid of leaving you. My sisters have their families and Mari has Charlie and the kids. I didn't worry about them. Their lives will go on without me. But you…I worried you would forever be alone."

"Mom—"

"Hush, I'm trying to get my deathbed confession out."

I shut my mouth with a smile on my face. How the woman could make me smile even now, at a time like this. I grabbed the damn tissue box and held it in my lap, afraid the tears might spill over onto my cheek.

"Mari has a good husband and beautiful children. So do my sisters. But do you know what they don't have?"

I shook my head.

"None of them ever found the love or the passion I had with your father. I know what you're thinking. But Alejandro loved me with great passion, just as he loved his country. And this isn't about Alejandro's choice, it's about mine." She stopped to catch her breath. I caught a tear with a tissue before it rolled down her cheek.

"I've loved your father every day of my life since I met him, and I will continue to love him until my last." Her voice was so soft now I had to lean almost against her to hear. "You asked me once why I didn't find someone else. There was no one else. Not for me. I couldn't settle for anything less. I didn't want to."

She turned her head toward me, and I leaned closer in so she could kiss my cheek. "You're part your father, Jared—charming, beautiful, and passionate. But you're also part me, and your love, once given, will last a lifetime."

She reached for my hand. "She loves you the same way, son. I've seen it."

"I hope so, Mom." My voice cracked.

"I know so, and now that I've met her, I know you'll be fine."

"We'll be fine." I ended the struggle over my tears and let them come.

Her hand tightened, and her gaze burned into mine. "Don't let her get away, son." Her eyes began to close. Her breaths became shallower and softer. "I love you, honey."

The last word could have been just a breath, and mine was as quiet as hers. "Love you too."

Her hand went slack. The monitor flat-lined.

Chapter Twenty-Three

Violet

I shook awake and sat bolt up in bed.

"Violet."

It wasn't until Jared said my name that I realized it was him shaking me awake, and from the look on his face, I didn't have to ask why.

"She's gone." I stated, my voice breaking on the words.

"She's gone," he agreed.

"I'm so sorry, Jared."

"So am I." He dragged me out of the top bunk and held me, my feet dangling above the floor.

"What time is it?"

"A little after two."

My arms laced around his neck, and I rested my head on his chest. "Is there anything you need me to do?"

"No. Just be with me. Mari went home to Charlie and the kids. Marvis is taking care of things. Aunt Penny and Aunt Julie went back to their hotel to get a few hours of sleep before we make arrangements in the morning."

"And you were wandering the house alone?"

He nodded.

I gave him a watery smile. "Then I'm glad you woke me."

"Actually, I just wanted to move you."

"Move me? Where?"

"Down here. With me." He laid me on the bottom bunk and slid in behind me. "I want to hold you, Violet."

"That sounds like a plan to me."

I let him wrap his arms around me and draw me close. His body wasn't as warm as it normally was. My hands rested against his chest, and I snuggled in closer to give him some of my heat. He shook and trembled under my touch.

I lay encircled in his arms for a long while. Eventually his body stopped quivering, and his breaths went in and out evenly. I let my own body relax and tried not to think of what he'd lost tonight, what we'd all lost.

****

I swam in a sea of sorrow. Warmth and sadness engulfed me.

A quiet rough sob filtered through the haze of my dreams, and slowly I came back to awareness.

I'd fallen asleep in Jared's bed. He was holding me so tight and was crying so hard his tears had moistened the pillow.

My heart clenched and broke. My hand came up to stroke the hair back from his wet cheek. "Oh, honey, I'm so sorry."

He wrapped me up tighter and let out an anguished cry, rocking me back and forth for several minutes. He pulled back and looked into my eyes, his handsome features ravaged by grief. Even in the dark room I could see that red rimmed the fathomless brown. Vulnerability and brokenness were two things I never expected to see in his gaze and two things I never wanted to see there again. I cupped his cheek and whispered, "What can I do?"

He stared at me for a long time, tracing the outline of my face with his gaze. Anguish and grief were joined by flame and desire. When his gaze met mine, his unspoken declaration was clear: *Let me make love to you.*

That was what he needed. I saw it in his face, in his eyes. He wasn't pretending. Neither could I. The raw need and desire shone like the sun. He was offering up his shattered, grief-stricken heart right here in this twin bed, and though I didn't have to, I wanted to give him my whole, untried, unbroken heart in return. I threaded my fingers in the hair at the nape of his neck and pulled him closer.

It was all the assent he needed. He swooped down on me like an avenging angel. The tenderness of the moment gave way to a devouring frenzy. His lips engulfed mine, his tongue thrusting hot and slick. There was no teasing, no seduction, just need. Desire rolled off of him and broke over me in stormy waves.

He rolled me to my back and was over me in an instant, my gown pulled over my head and tossed aside. He kissed down my neck, my chest, to my breasts, licking and biting in lush, generous strokes, leaving a wet trail chilled by the air. He steadied one breast with a warm, deft hand and bent to take my nipple in his mouth, sucking roughly. A keening cry flew from my lips and my back arched up into him. Finally my desire matched his, and I gave in, running my hands over his shoulders, down his back.

That seemed to drive him more urgently. He laved and sucked, worshipping my body like it was his salvation. My heart felt like it would beat out of my chest. Every inch of my skin heated. My toes burned in the fuzzy socks as he inched down my belly until he reached my pelvic bone.

On his knees between my spread legs, he rested, drawing in sharp breaths. His heavy-lidded eyes opened fully, and he looked up from between my thighs like the devil himself. His long lashes were still wet with tears. He leisurely slipped his fingers under the elastic waistband of my panties and curled those naughty digits into a tight grip on the fabric. None of the urgency left his gaze, but his movements were measured.

"Oh God." The space throbbed in painful anticipation. I'd never needed a man so desperately, so violently it hurt, but tonight I did.

He slid my panties slowly down my legs, never once breaking our gaze. The intense sexual power of him overwhelmed me like a helpless ship tossed in a hurricane. He winced as if the deliberate unhurried way he was undressing me was costing him, killing him, but he kept the steady pace.

I pulled my legs up when he got the panties past my thighs. Finally, he jerked them off and tossed them on the floor. A salacious smile covered his deep red lips as he looked down at my body. He licked those lips and ran a lazy finger through the folds of my sex. It slid with embarrassing ease through the wetness. I whimpered. Nothing so excruciating had ever felt so good. I was on the edge of a sea-swept cliff looking straight down into disaster, but I couldn't stop. There was no way I could stop.

He stripped off his T-shirt and pajama bottoms. Then he was between my thighs, his mouth hot and searching against my lips. The enflamed skin of our bodies touched at every possible point. He rocked his hardness against me. I moaned loudly into his plunging kiss. He pumped himself between the slickened folds below, preparing for penetration. I knew he would thrust hard and quick. The escalation of this last week was in his kiss. The current of unfettered emotion had receded and was building behind a wave in a tidal storm.

My hazy brain flickered. *"Jared."* The word was so breathy I wasn't sure if he'd heard or understood.

He pulled back to look at me.

"Condom" was all I could get out.

He went completely still, his face filling with emotion. "I don't have one, Vi." His arms, braced on either side of my head, quivered with strain and need. His jaw clenched. "Please."

It was a whispered plea.

His eyes filled with tears. "I swear to God, Violet, I'm clean. If you get pregnant, I'll take care of you." A tear ran down his cheek and dropped onto mine. *"Please."* The desperation of the word held for single heartbeat.

I couldn't deny him. In that moment and forever after, I'd give him anything, everything. I felt tears stream down my own face and into my ears. I nodded once and whispered, "Take me."

He did, and my heart was his.

Chapter Twenty-Four

Jared

The first light of dawn filtered between the blinds and made the red in Violet's hair shimmer like a new penny. I gently brushed a few strands from her face. She stirred in peaceful sleep.

A wave of tenderness and sorrow engulfed me. An ache and an emptiness crushed my chest, but it wasn't a new emptiness. It was a new awareness of what had always been there. It was a life without permanence, without someone to share it, and without someone to love.

Violet could fill that place, and after what we shared last night, I believed she would.

For the first time in my life I had reached out to a woman in love, and she'd responded. It was like the first time. For me, sex had never been about emotion, had never touched my heart. Until last night. The bond Violet and I had shared, the intimacy, went beyond bare skin into raw emotion. Finally something real. Something of substance, and something that would last.

Christ, I was maudlin this morning. I shook my head and couldn't help but chuckle at myself. What a waste my life had been, waiting for a woman who had never understood me and a man who had given me his genetics but nothing else.

Now that I had lost the one person who had unconditionally loved me, I realized what a void it created. But last night Mom had helped me realize it wasn't the void of being unloved that caused my problems, but the horde of love I had refused to give. That was the bigger issue. An issue I intended to remedy.

That was what Mom wanted, and I finally understood, after all these years, it was what I wanted too.

I gently pulled my arm from behind Violet's head and slipped from the bed, down the hall and into the shower.

After a steaming soak, my mind cleared and the smell of coffee drowned out my other senses. I trod to the kitchen toward the siren call of caffeine.

"Jared. You're up." Alex stood at the sink washing dishes and Mrs. C peeked in on something cooking in the oven. She turned down the dial.

"Both casseroles are done, Al."

Alex opened the cabinet and placed the dish she'd just dried on the shelf. She turned to face me, looking more than a little guilty. "We thought we'd make breakfast for you. Mari called us last night."

Neither of them mentioned Mom, but thoughts of her hung between us.

Mrs. C wiped her hands on her apron and pulled my cheek down for a kiss and a brisk hug. "It will be a long day of arrangements. You can use a little nourishment. We were hoping to get in and out before you woke up." She grabbed a box of utensils and headed toward the back door. "There's cowboy casserole with eggs, bacon, sausage, and cheese, and French toast casserole. Help yourself, sweetheart." She turned back to gaze at her daughter. "Are you coming?"

Alex nodded. "In a minute."

Mrs. C cradled her box in one arm as she opened the door with the other. "Let us know about the arrangements, and I'll get the word out, Jared."

"Thanks, Mrs. C."

She smiled but a tear ran down her cheek as she closed the door. My own eyes stung and I scrubbed my face with my hands.

"How do you like your coffee?"

"Black."

Alex poured me a cup and picked up her own. "You want to come talk in the living room?"

"Sure." I followed her in.

It was where Mom always went in the morning with her coffee. How many times had she sat on this couch with her mug and her paper?

Alex set her cup on the table and scooted toward me. "I can't believe she's gone, Jared. I loved her."

"I know you did."

"She was such a huge influence on me—almost as much as my own mother." She glanced up with teary eyes. "I'm sorry. I should be comforting you."

"It's okay. It's good to know others appreciated her and saw her for the amazing woman she was." I pulled Alex into my chest and she rested there, dainty and warm.

"Do you remember that time she helped us build the pyramids for our social studies class?"

I laughed. "And we vacuumed sand out of the carpet for weeks."

Her body shook with a small chuckle. "Except where you'd spilled the glue."

"Mom never minded. Even after a long day of cleaning hotel rooms she would always come in and help. She never complained."

"No. She was always happy. She led a happy life." Alex sighed. She craned her neck to look up at me. "I regret not spending more time with her."

"Me too," I agreed.

"I regret a lot of things, Jared." She pulled back to look at me, love filling her eyes. "I've always loved you, and now I'll never have a chance to show you."

I gulped down the awkward knot in my throat. "No."

"Can you honestly tell me you don't love me, Jared?"

"Of course I can't. I'll always love you, Alex, but not…" I didn't know how to say it without sounding trite, without using the same words I'd used with girls who'd said they loved me over the years. I didn't want to give her those. She deserved better, but she deserved the truth. My heart belonged to another.

She took my hand. "You don't have to say it. I understand. I wish it was different."

I shook my head, realizing for the first time that I didn't. "No. You don't, Alex. You have your daughter. You'll find someone who loves you like you deserve to be loved."

"I hope so." A look of resignation crossed her face. Then she eyed me speculatively. "But I'll always wonder what would've happened…"

She leaned in toward me, her voice a whisper. "I'm going to kiss you, Jared. I've wanted to since I was thirteen years old. Please let me."

I didn't say yes, but I didn't stop her either, and before I could take a breath, her lips touched mine. It was a soft sweet kiss of innocence and memories and it was over almost before it began.

Alex sighed. "Be happy, Jarry."

"You too." My arms went around her and we hugged for a long time.

She pulled away and stood. "Don't let your coffee get cold, and call us if you need anything."

Then she was gone.

Chapter Twenty-Five

Violet

This time, the cries of the gulls woke me. I cracked my eyes open and slivers of sun filtered in.

I was alone in the room. But not in the house.

The murmur of voices and clink of coffee cups told me the family had arrived. A great pounding ache hit my chest. Cathy was gone, and I would never see her smile or hear her stories again. I winced as I sat up, the space between my legs tender and sore.

Oh my God. Jared. He'd made love to me so ferociously. I'd read about that wild, abandoned sort of sex but never believed it could be real. Every atom of our beings had engaged. His hunger and need had driven me, and we'd propelled each other. It sounded hokey as I thought it, but that was the truth. Single-minded in his quest, he'd been generous, making sure I experienced the heights with him. And we had soared. Above pain, heartbreak, fear of the past and the future.

It was no small wonder why women fluttered and flocked to him. Mari's words came back: *Jared's a strong partner.*

And not just in dancing. But it was how he'd given himself. Almost as if he'd opened his heart and poured the contents inside of me. Was that how he always did it? Was that how he fooled them into believing he was theirs?

I couldn't believe that. I wouldn't believe it. What we had was too raw and real. What I'd experienced was the real Jared. There had been no barriers. No protection. It had been reckless. We could've conceived a child—Jared's child. The thought didn't disturb me as much as it should've. In fact, it gave me hope, and hope was what we all needed this morning.

I tumbled out of the bottom bunk, cool air hitting my naked body. I snatched up fresh clothes and pulled them on. What would this day bring? I knew what it would be like. I remembered. A parent's funeral is something you never forget, no matter how young.

Shades and shadows of my father's flashed in my mind as I brushed tangles from my hair. It was as if Cathy's passing had opened the chest of photo albums, and my mind was allowing me access to long-forgotten memories.

I stepped out of the bedroom. A quiet cloud hung over the house. Jared's murmur resonated down the hall and made me pause. I couldn't make out the words but the tone was clear.

A woman laughed softly. Probably Mari. Then she spoke in low tones. But it wasn't Mari… I turned my ear toward the sound. Maybe it was an aunt.

I padded on with silent steps and peered around the corner.

He was talking with…Alex. And then he was holding her, leaning in to—

Oh, God. They were kissing.

I jerked my head back. I didn't need to watch anymore. I knew the ending to this movie because it was a bad remake. I should've listened to Luke and Lucy. Why had I let him in? Why? I knew better.

A big neon sign should be blinking over my head: World's Most Colossal Idiot. "I was warned."

I spun around to find Mari watching the scene over my shoulder.

She shook her head at her brother in disgust. "He's a fool, Violet. He always has been when it comes to Alex. I'm sorry."

I ran back to the room, grabbed my bag, and shoved my clothes in. Where would I go? How could I extricate myself without a scene? My God. I didn't want to be one of his women who caused a scene. The pitiful ones.

I folded my pajamas and dropped them in, but shook my head.

I had to stay for the funeral. I owed Cathy that. Her son I owed nothing, except a kick in the groin.

"No. That's not right." I tossed my toiletry bag in the carry-on. Why should I blame Jared? Was it really his fault? I'd known going in—and still I fell. "Idiot!"

I shoved in a pair of flip-flops.

"Going somewhere?"

The seductive voice slid up my spine. Damn him. I would not play the jealous, hurt, pitiful fool. Last night had been sympathy sex. I'd provided a service, nothing more. Pain ripped at my heart and tears threatened to fall. I'd given him everything last night, and I couldn't take it back if I'd wanted to. For the record, I did want to.

"Violet? Bags? Why are you packing?"

I took a deep breath. I couldn't stay here, and I couldn't leave. Conundrum. I needed Mom. The one person who could help me get through this. Light dawned in my addled brain. That was my answer and my excuse.

I pasted on an air of calm and prayed my words made sense—even if nothing else did. "My mom is coming for the funeral. She wanted to be here to pay her respects. I've got a car coming to take me to Mr. Scorge's hotel. She and I will stay there tonight so you and your family can have room and privacy."

A flicker of hurt flashed in his eyes. "I thought you'd stay with me."

I couldn't cave. It was an act. I'd heard the lies before. I'd been on his end of many such telephone conversations. I knew how he operated. "Jared, you know I don't really belong here, and I need my own mother."

I hadn't intended that to be a slap, but he recoiled as if it was. His face hardened. He nodded. "Suit yourself." Then he left.

I picked up the phone as tears leaked down my face.

"Mom, I need you."

Chapter Twenty-Six

Violet

Mom lifted her chin. "You are my daughter. You can do this."

I put on a brave smile and walked into the funeral home. My legs wobbled and a knot the size of a speedboat stuck in my throat. My heart pounded out an anxious beat.

Mari stood near the door, talking in hushed tones to Charlie and Penny. Uncle Ed grabbed me. "There's my girl. How are you, blossom?"

"I'm hanging in there. Uncle Ed, this is my mother, Rose Murphy."

"Whew. I see where you get your good looks from."

Mom chuckled. "It's good to meet you, but so sorry for the circumstances."

Ed's smile slipped. "It's a loss." His lips thinned to a tight line, holding back strong emotion. He shook his head. "One we'll feel for a long time."

Mari caught sight of me and hurried over. She took my hands. "It wasn't what we thought, Violet. Give him a chance to explain."

"I'm sure he will once he gets back to work."

Understanding dawned on her. "You're not staying. After the funeral."

"No, I'm not staying. I need to get back to Chicago. This is my mother, Rose."

Mari grabbed my mother and pulled her into the tightest hug. "I'm only hugging you because my family has laid claim to your daughter and I feel we should give you something in return."

Mom chuckled softly. "Violet is definitely worth a hug."

Mari caught sight of something or someone behind us. Her face fell and her shoulders sagged under the weight of the day. "He needs you, Violet. Please come sit with us in the family section."

"I don't think I should do that." I wrapped my arms around her. "I know you have a strong support group, but if you need anything, please let me know."

"No." She shook her head and smiled. "It's not me who needs you, but I'm not going to ask for his sake. He has his own decisions to make." She met my gaze. "But thank you for being here now—and before."

Knots that had tightened in my stomach made their way to my throat. I couldn't speak. I squeezed her tight. She had become a friend, and in a small way, family.

I introduced Mom to Penny and Julie. They pointed out their various husbands, children, and grandchildren, none of whom Mom or I would ever meet again. Jared was nowhere to be seen. I scanned the crowd and found Marvis, Mabel, and Josie sitting together. Mom and I headed over to them.

The organ music began, and we took a seat near the aisle. I settled in, scanning the room, looking for people I recognized. I saw many.

In two weeks, Cathy had taken me into her family and her life. Even though she had so little to give, she gave her precious time to me, and I had taken it. There were more people than I'd expected. She had touched so many lives.

I craned my head toward the back of the chapel. Alex and her parents filed in and sat near the back. Seeing her was a jolt. Her blonde hair was pulled back into a smart ponytail and her black linen dress offset her complexion. She wore silver jewelry. Would she ever wear Cathy's ring?

That was a line of thought I refused to entertain today. This wasn't about Alex. Or even me. It was about Cathy.

Finally, as the family was led in, I saw Jared next to Corey with a space between him and Ava. An invisible rope tugged at my heart, pulling me toward him. I couldn't see his face, but I knew he needed me. I knew by the set of his jaw and shoulders. That space was for me.

I touched Mom's arm. "I have to go."

She nodded in understanding.

In a gesture of love and respect for the woman I'd grown to know and care for, and for her son, with whom I was hopelessly and helplessly in love, I made my way to the space reserved for me. Charlie and Mari stood to let me into the row. I slipped by Ava and sat next to her with Jared on my other side.

A small, relieved exhalation blew from his lips. He never turned his head, but his hand grabbed mine, and he tightly laced our fingers.

The service wasn't long but reverent and beautiful. After the last song played and the family rose, Jared pulled me up and together we walked past the casket.

Outside the warm mid-summer sun beat down. The family had decided against a graveside service. Everyone was headed back to the house for a catered lunch.

Jared never met my gaze. "You aren't coming back to the house."

He hadn't phrased it as a question, and I got the impression he hadn't asked because he couldn't bear the answer if I'd refused.

I wouldn't have refused him. Not today.

He'd hurt me, and he had things to explain. He had decisions to make. About Alex, and about me. But I wouldn't have left him if he'd asked me to stay.

He didn't ask.

"I'm taking Mom back to the hotel. We have a flight out this evening."

Scanning some place out in the distance, he nodded once. "Have a safe trip. I'll see you next week."

He turned on his heel, walked over to a weeping Alex, took her in his arms.

My heart broke, and I went home.

Chapter Twenty-Seven

Violet

"Hi, Violet."

The greetings came as I marched stoically to my desk.

"Nice to have you back."

I plastered on a smile. "Good to be back."

I wasn't sure how any of this mess with Jared would work. I flipped on my computer. But I refused to be another notch on his desk. Another assistant he'd screwed and left. Nope. Not gonna be me all weepy and brokenhearted.

My email, which was also connected to Jared's, came up on the start screen. Four hundred messages. I'd be here all week weeding through it.

My coffee in hand, I was ready. I scanned the files for junk mail. That was nearly half. Jared's entourage had sent more than seventy. I deleted those. The remaining messages were from legitimate sources. So I began to weed through. Mr. Tate had sent a long series of email to Scorge and copied Jared. The marketing manager had sent daily reports, so I could get rid of those.

Now what did we have here?

From: Dr. Simon Huxtley

Re: Results of DataMatch profile

Alexis Callahan-Burns: We found a perfect position in accounting for her.

Hux

There was an attachment too: an excel spreadsheet titled *Results*.

I clicked on it, my heart pounding in my ears. Rows and rows of numbers and percentages filled the pages. I scrolled down to the last two, where there were categories containing overall percentages.

Family: 99.75%

Life Goals: 91.63%

Attraction and Body Chem: 96.54%

Spatial Reasoning Function: 99.32%

And on and on it went. With each line my heart shattered into smaller and smaller pieces. Until I came to the end.

Overall Compatibility: 98.34%

Pain stabbed my heart. A groan spilled from my lips. Alex was his perfect match and now she was moving to Chicago.

And why shouldn't she move here?

She was the one who was meant to be with Jared. She knew him better, had grown up with him, had known his family, their struggles. She belonged in his life. Not me.

And then I did what I swore I would *never* do. I became the weepy assistant who resigned. Through sobs and tears, I typed the letter and sent it to Nathaniel Scorge.

As soon as I'd sent it, I heard a gasp from down the hall. Maddie's head jerked from her computer screen back to me. She typed in a quick email before hurrying over.

I shoved from my desk and rushed into Jared's office so I could fall apart in peace.

She followed. "Oh no, you don't." She closed the door softly behind her. "What did he do?"

I sobbed into her shirt as her arms came around me. Between cries, I got out, "He's in love with someone else."

"Who could he possibly be in love with besides you, Violet?" Her question was gentle. She pulled back to look at my face. Wincing, Maddie scurried out to my desk for tissue, not even bothering to look in Jared's. When she came back in, she sat me down on his sofa. "I've seen him with you, Violet. He feels something different for you than the others. That is certain. He would've never invited you there if he hadn't cared."

A soft chuckle escaped me. "That's almost exactly what his mother said."

"So you got along well with his family."

That started a whole new round of tears. I nodded. "Very well."

I couldn't imagine never seeing them again. Watching Mari's kids grow up, and listening to Uncle Ed's jokes. But mostly I'd miss sitting at the kitchen table, drinking a cup of coffee with Cathy. It wasn't just Jared who'd stolen my heart. It was all of them.

Shortly after, Lucy followed by Luke stormed in.

"Where is he?" Luke fisted his hands.

"Hold back there, Manny Pacquiao." Lucy grabbed his flexing bicep. "Let's hear the evidence before we rush to judgment."

Just like a typical lawyer.

Settling into Jared's informal seating area, I told them the whole story. I explained about Alexis, Cathy, and Jared's family. I told them about the talent show, and her passing. I shared everything. Well, I left out a couple of key ingredients like Alejandro and the dance club, but they caught the subtext without me having to give the details.

They all sat there, silent, just blinking, unable to speak. Maddie and I swiped away tears. Lucy dotted the corner of her eyes with a tissue. Even Luke's face lined with sympathy for Jared.

"So you see. It's not his fault." I shook my head. "It's just the way it is."

Lucy threw up her arms. "I can't believe he did this again. Like that." She frowned. "He's still culpable, Vi. He had no right using you, taking your heart when he needed it and tossing it away the next."

While Lucy's perspective might have been colored by the past, she had a good point. "That's true. But the damage is done."

"It doesn't surprise me that he used you. Cassidy is a taker, not a giver, and he always will be," Luke tossed out.

"No. That isn't Jared. That isn't who he is." I had visions of Jared building that platform in the backyard, helping his mother, playing with his nieces and nephews, teaching me yoga and Latin dance. I shook my head. He wasn't just a taker. With his family and with me, he'd given what he had. He just didn't love me, and I couldn't fault him for that. I fought down the lump in my throat. "The fact remains that I'm in love with him and I always will be." My voice broke. "And because of that I can't work here anymore."

Lucy fired off at me, "You can't do this. You can't let him do this to you."

Maddie grabbed my hand and shoved another stack of tissues in it.

"I knew it!" Luke paced in front of me. He glanced up at Lucy and me sitting in Jared's office. "This is the exact same thing he did to Lucy. I'll kill him."

I knew Luke was angrier with Jared for what Jared had done to Lucy than to me, but I loved the fact that he wanted to play protector.

But he couldn't protect me from how I felt. Nobody could, and that was why I had to leave.

Chapter Twenty-Eight

Jared

The sound of the surf crashed around me. I dug my hands into the sand. I didn't even know how long I'd been sitting out here with my knees bent and my palms braced behind me. The sun had set and the stars were twinkling in the darkening sky. It had been two long days since the funeral.

"Brought you a beer."

I looked up at Nathaniel and took the bottle from him. "The family still up there?"

"A few, but most have gone." He sat next to me. "How you holding up?"

There was no need to mince words with my oldest friend and business partner. "Glad it's all over."

"Yeah."

"Now we just have to clear out the stuff."

"Are you going to sell the house?"

"Don't know yet. Mari wants to keep it. Maybe rent it out."

We sat there for a while watching the surf.

Nathaniel spoke. "You know I came to see her a few months ago. After the deal with Tate."

I dangled my beer loosely between my legs and looked over at him, unable to hide the surprise from my face. "Didn't know."

I wasn't surprised that Nathaniel had sought out Mom for answers. He'd done that before—ever since we were kids. She had been the closest thing to a mother he'd had growing up. But I was surprised she hadn't told me.

He propped his hands on his bent knees. "She gave me some sound advice about Maddie."

"Advice was always her specialty." The truth of that statement rang out. I took a drink. I counted on her wisdom for so many things and now I was on my own. We all were. "What did she tell you?"

"Said I had to let her go. Let her see if she could be happier with…*him*." He spat out the word like it was bad seafood.

"Can you do that?"

"Not sure, but I promised I'd try. If I can do it, I ought to win a damn medal." Nathaniel took a swig of his own beer. "We set out to prove the DataMatch program was accurate."

"Guess we've done that."

"So far." He paused and took a deep breath. "What about you and Violet?"

"What about us?" My heart began to rev. I hadn't meant for the statement to sound so defensive. I knew I had some clean up to do with her. She'd left without giving me a chance to explain. That had hurt, but with my past I could hardly blame her. The truth was, I never should've let Alex have that kiss. It was a mistake.

After we got Mom's affairs in order and I headed back to Chicago, Violet and I were going to sit down and have a long discussion about us and our future.

"She turned in her notice today. I got the email."

"She's not leaving."

"She thinks she is."

"She's wrong."

"Okay." Nathaniel seemed satisfied. He stood and dusted the sand from his pant leg. "See you back at the house."

I nodded. Guess I had some work cut out for me.

Chapter Twenty-Nine

Violet

"You bastard. You would've let me marry someone else?"

Jared's silky tenor sent shivers over me. Reminisces of *Ravished by a Rogue* returned with ironic vengeance. "I still would, and keep away from my romance novels."

He tramped farther into the office. "I'm back."

"Whoop dee doo." I would not cry over this. Looking up from his desk, I finally caught sight of him, which was a bad move. His hair was as well cut as his suit, but he had dark circles under his eyes. My heart melted.

No—he was a lame-ass, lying sack of crap. I turned away and continued to move around his office, straightening things that possibly needed it.

He grabbed hold of my arm. "Damn it, Vi. Look at me."

I turned my head as far away as I could without breaking my own neck.

"Please."

"Let me go." I jerked my arm free and completely turned my back on him.

"I can't do that."

"Why not?"

"I'm in love with you."

I could feel his grin on my shoulder blades, could see it in my mind's eye. He wasn't serious. He was quoting *Moonstruck.*

He sighed. "Come on. Aren't you even gonna take the opportunity to slap me and say, 'Snap out of it?'"

I didn't budge. He'd hurt me too much for me to make light of this.

He walked around, coming face to face with me. "I didn't kiss Alex. She kissed me. Then she apologized."

I studied my toes. I needed a pedicure.

He lifted my chin. "'I'm just a boy—'"

"If you say, 'I'm just a boy standing in front of a girl, asking her to love him,' I will kick you in the testicles and walk out this minute."

He pouted like a petulant child. "You're walking out in two weeks anyway. Nathaniel told me you turned in your notice." He stuffed his hands in his pockets, looking truly confused and grieved. "I thought romance was what you wanted."

"That was what I used to want, but I'm tired of watching someone else's love story unfold." I raked him from head to toe with my gaze. "And I'm not keen on the story I was written into, so I'll go find another. According to the good Dr. Huxtley, it's all a matter of numbers."

Jealousy flashed in his eyes. *"No."*

"Why shouldn't I find someone?" Was he going to fight for me? A glimmer of hope sprang up inside of me. I was an idiot.

"No, Vi. You can't."

Something in my chest began to thaw, and I didn't want it to. Hope, the damned eternal stuff. I wanted to be angry and hateful and say mean hurtful things. "Why not?"

He stepped closer. (I let him—I want to make that perfectly clear.) "Because you'll never find anyone better than me."

I deflated like a cheap beach float. I should've known this was only about his pride. It was about how he didn't want *his match* to get away while everyone else got theirs.

"Because…" He took his hands out of his pockets and touched my cheek, the look on his face nailing me to the spot. "I love you, Violet, and I can't live without you."

I scanned the files of my brain and couldn't match the scene. I locked my knees so I wouldn't sink to the carpet. Who knew what had happened on that stuff? It was *Jared's* office, after all. But if my legs were the consistency of memory foam, my knees were only slightly better. I began to descend.

He grabbed my elbow and pulled me against him. His arms wrapped around me, warmth and strength seeping in where I was most vulnerable. "Did you hear me, blossom? I love you."

I wouldn't give in that easily. "And you expect me to fall into your arms?"

He gave me a brief once-over and shrugged matter-of-factly.

Well, it wasn't going to be that easy. Not after what he'd done. I conjured up the memory of him sitting on the sofa, comforting another girl—a girl he still loved—hours after I'd given him everything I had. Pain and humiliation flooded back. Nothing like a good dose of that to get my blood pumping and alleviate the symptoms of lovesickness.

I pushed away from him again. "Not this time, Casanova. I'm not charmed. Not anymore. Because I know all your tricks." I straightened my shoulders and stared up at him with as much indifference as I could scrape together.

"You know why I only date girls once or twice?"

"Because you get bored," I said, knowing it was a lie. I knew the reason. I knew him.

"Because I don't let myself get attached. I move on to the next one as soon as I begin to feel." His thumb caressed my cheek in soft little circles. "There's no moving on this time, Violet. I'm caught." His gaze searched mine and his voice cracked as he said, "I'm home. For me, this is the end of the road. You're the end of a long journey."

"I'm sure you can convince Alexis to take you. Go find her. She's your 98.3 percent match. And apparently a good kisser."

"You know good and well that was her kiss not mine."

I actually did know that. Jared had called me two days after the funeral to explain, but because I wouldn't pick up, he emailed it to me, texted it, and left me a voicemail at home and work.

"And what are you talking about, 'perfect match'?" He frowned and squinted his eyes. "Alexis isn't my match."

"Yes, she is." I propped my hand on my hips.

"No, she isn't."

"Yes."

"No."

"I heard you ask Hux to run the numbers. I saw the DataMatch results."

"Those results were for you, Violet. Alexis was a fifty-five-percent match. Not even worth exploring as far as the computer was concerned." He humphed and shook his head.

Fifty-five percent? Could that be right?

"All these years. Wasted years. That damned computer knew my heart before I did." He stepped closer again. (And just so everyone knows, I let him—again.) "There's no one else, Violet. I'm not looking anymore." Tears, honesty, and, I swear to God, love glinted in his eyes.

My own eyes seemed a little watery, but I stalwartly held them at bay.

"Go if you have to. Make me wait if you must." He took a shaky breath and ran his thumb over my lips with such tenderness. His eyes locked with mine. "But I swear...on my mother's grave."

My hand flew to my mouth, holding back a gasp.

"I will never love another woman more than I love you, Violet Murphy." A tear rolled down his cheek in a little trail and one of mine followed. He threw his head back and cleared his throat, then went to his desk, grabbed the package he'd dropped, and handed it to me.

Tentatively, I took it from him and pulled the ribbon that bound the paper around the soft object inside. The brown wrapping fell open, revealing the antique lace tablecloth and a note that read: *I still want you to have this. Give it a chance, blossom. —Cathy*

"*An Affair to Remember.*" My chest tightened. My heart ached, and more tears fell. "She did this for me?"

"No." He met my surprised gaze. "She did it for me. For us. It was wrapped up in my box of things with this." From his suit pocket he pulled out his own folded note and a little velvet pouch fell with it. The contents jingled.

A heavy lump formed in my throat.

I took the paper.

Alejandro's tablecloth is for Violet. These are for you to get both of them back.

In his palm lay Cathy's engagement ring and wedding band.

The lump in my throat knotted. A watery smile formed on his lips. That smile ripped at my bound-up heart. He plucked the rings from their nesting place and bent his knee to kneel, but then suddenly stopped. "Oh. Wait. I almost forgot."

A shaky hand withdrew his phone from his jacket pocket. He tapped on the touch screen, then once again bent to one knee, this time making it all the way to the floor. "Will you Violet Elizabeth Murphy..."

All your life you've waited...for love to come and stay...

"The Goodbye Girl" began to play. My hand flew to my mouth, stifling a mingled cry and a giggle, and I couldn't see for the blasted tears.

He laughed too. "Will you marry me?"

"You're crazy, you know that?" Tears, snot, a little sweat ran down my face. It was the most romantic moment of my life.

"I am. About you. So…will you?"

I gazed at the ring offered up in his hand. It was the perfect proposal. Perfect for me. I knuckled away several more tears and sniffed. "I guess I could do that."

"Good." He slipped it on my finger and stood. "You won't get the other ring unless you follow through, you know."

I nodded. "I know."

He pushed a lock of my hair behind my ear. "Are you sure you can handle being stuck with me for the rest of your life?"

"It sure beats being stuck without you." I looked at his phone on the desk, the song still playing. "So you're saying good-bye?"

He shook his head and wrapped me in his arms. He whispered kisses over my cheeks and lips and neck. "Not a chance." Then he lifted his head and arched his sexy eyebrow. "But I *could* sing along."

I snickered. "I'd rather you didn't."

"I thought I warned you to leave her alone."

Both our heads jerked toward the door where, unbeknownst to us, a small crowd had gathered. Luke stormed in.

I threw my body in front of Jared, and the big sissy cowered behind me. "It's okay, Luke."

The man stopped and said, "Okay my ass." Then he started toward us again.

Jared stepped out from around me. "I've asked Violet to marry me."

That stopped Luke in his tracks. "Tell me you didn't say yes." He glanced at my hand. "Jesus, Violet. Are you really gonna fall for this joker?"

"I already have." A wide grin spread over my face. "He's not as bad as you think."

"Really? I seem to remember you balling your eyes out in this office over him two days ago."

"*Him* is standing right here." Jared held out his arms. Then he narrowed his eyes. "Wait." He turned toward me. "You were balling your eyes out?"

I shrugged.

He frowned and pulled me into a big hug. "I'm so sorry, blossom." He squeezed me tight, cupping my head to his chest. "I can't promise never to make you ball your eyes out again—it is me we're talking about—but I promise to never again make you do it alone." He pulled back and gazed into my face. "I love you, Violet."

My knees gave way again. He caught me before I slipped and kissed me deeply. My mouth opened. His tongue swept inside. My arms laced around his neck and he bent me back in a romantic dip. I sighed and pushed up into his kiss.

Jared lifted his head. "What are you still doing here, Luck? Get out. This ain't no peep show."

I turned to find Luke looking like he'd been hit over the head. He blinked then scanned the air with a wince. "What the hell is this music?"

Jared nearly dropped me on my butt, but steadied me and fumbled for his phone, pressing the music off. "Celine Dion. 'My Heart Will Go On.'" He looked guiltily back and forth between Luke and me. "What? I just thought if David Gates didn't work, the theme from *Titanic* might."

Luke shook his head and turned to leave. "That's pathetic, man."

Jared pouted as we watched Luke shut the door behind him. "It wasn't pathetic. It was supposed to be romantic."

I laced my arms around his neck. "It is romantic."

I pressed the music on, pulled his head toward me, and before I kissed him, said, "I love you."

And I knew it was the most romantic moment of his life.

ABOUT THE AUTHOR

Kary Rader is an award-winning author, stay-at-home mom, and part-time Twitter sage, because one shouldn't have to use more than 140 characters to impart wisdom. She lives with her husband, three kids, and one low-maintenance kitty cat in the Dallas/Fort Worth metroplex. Whether contemporary or fantasy, spicy or sweet, her stories always have true love, romance, and lots of humor.

Did you enjoy this book? Drop us a line and say so! We love to hear from readers, and so do our authors. To connect, visit www.boroughspublishinggroup.com online, send comments directly to info@boroughspublishinggroup.com, or friend us on Facebook and Twitter. And be sure to check back regularly for contests and new releases in your favorite subgenres of romance!

Are you an aspiring writer? Check out www.boroughspublishinggroup.com/submit and see if we can help you make your dreams come true.

www.ingramcontent.com/pod-product-compliance
Lightning Source LLC
Chambersburg PA
CBHW060618130626
46555CB00002B/554